With appreciation
   and gratefulness
   towards
   many people,
   animals and plants
   on the long way back
   to my own Self

For a
   beautiful world
   where
   our people
   of the
   one
   worldwide family
   may thrive
   in creativity and joy
   as a part
   of all creation

THE TANTRA CONNECTION

Healing Through Cosmic Interface

by

MONIKA MÜLLER

HARDBACK: 978-1-948779-01-2
PAPERBACK: 978-1-948779-00-5
EBOOK: 978-1-948779-02-9

Illustrations:
Monika Müller, Michelle Pochadt

Photo Front Cover: www.dreamstime

English language composition:
Telbisz van Dierendonck

Prior editions:
Self-publishing in Canada, Sherbrooke 2002, Montreal 2005, 2006
AuthorHouse, USA 2009

Ordering Information:

For orders and inquiries, please contact:
1-888-375-9818
www.toplinkpublishing.com
bookorder@toplinkpublishing.com

Printed in the United States of America

MY GRATITUDE AND LOVE GO
TO EVERYONE,
WHO CROSSED MY PATH
AND CAUSED ME
TO FEEL AND THINK ABOUT LIFE
IN DEPTH.

MAY THEY ALWAYS THRIVE IN BEAUTY,
JOY AND LOVE,
FINDING COMPLETION IN THEIR SELF.

Table of Contents

Introduction

Until recently, the only way people were able to achieve a tantric way of life, was through the guidance of a guru, yogi, or yogini. Even those who were able to travel to ashrams or secluded areas to work with the Tantra masters did not always succeed in their efforts.

More than thirty-five years of unconventional life experiences have shown me that today many more of us are internally ready to walk the "tantric path". Yet, it is less than ever practical for thousands, perhaps even millions, to uproot their lives in the quest to reach conscious unity with the universal energy.

Living the essence of life, Tantra, can be achieved by anyone with determination.

Six virtues are fundamental to a tantric way of life:

- will-power
- courage to be
- love of life
- sense of humor
- confidence and trust
- willingness to surrender

All of us have these virtues within us, however in most of us they are dormant. Although the "tantric path" is much less challenging if one is already living them consciously, very few of us are at that level. Each step you take will bring you closer to awaking these six virtues within yourself.

We have been trained to think of **willpower** strictly in the sense of doing unpleasant things in order to achieve a goal. This kind of repression is not an element of Tantra. Positive willpower allows you to tap into the universal energy. This path equips you with the endurance and perseverance necessary to live beauty, deep joy, and life to the full.

For you to set sail with this positive willpower, **courage** will have to be your rudder. After all, when friends and family show good intentions in their attempts to include us in their world, it takes courage to seek inner mastery rather than follow the tides of fashion, or the flow of goods and services. The "tantric path" leads inward before it heads anywhere else, and it takes courage to follow your own way.

If you have taken the time to reflect upon your past, you will surely have understood the importance of letting go of suffering, and the need to free yourself of the "wounded child" in you. To be able to deal with your past you will need courage, as well as constant alertness in the present.

Your inner self will support you in this liberating process. At first it may be hard to distinguish your real inner self from all the other voices, which have over the years formed a steady stream of inner dialogue. These voices are a conglomerate of the opinions and value systems that have been imposed upon us by our parents, teachers, and even through peer pressure. These societal agents have an undo influence, of which we are hardly aware.

As you experience new ways of dealing with problems, your curiosity can help you to discover your "free inner child", and letting go of societal conditioning will become that much easier. Your courage to be, rather than to have, is the gateway to your "free inner child". Being yourself - not a confused image of yourself - will further stimulate your willpower and enhance your courage to follow this path. The wisdom of your "free inner child" will reveal your love.

Your desire to live the essence is rooted in your **love of life**. As you allow your "free inner child" to awaken your love of life, creativity becomes a natural state. This will help you replace heaviness, stagnation and repetition of old hurtful emotions with light-fullness, joy and laughter. You start to perceive the world in a "different light". Your love will not permit you to possess a person - it will open up and become universal, radiating more energy. As you reach this stage, a full appreciation of life blossoms.

Without a scent of optimism, no goal can be reached. Now that you have glimpsed light-fullness, since your "free inner child" has emerged, **humor** will fill the air. Feeling the capacity for a deep life-laughter enables you to laugh at yourself. This opens new dimensions and makes it much easier to look at yourself, consider your actions, and follow through on changes.

You will wonder about how past and present circumstances fit together. Perceiving the continuity of your life, the whole becomes evident, and so will the logic of it. If at this point laughter is not forthcoming, endless tears of relief may be the result.

A soupcon about the greater unity of all existence emerges.

To wonder is to begin to understand!

Without **confidence**, the journey into the unknown cannot be undertaken. Your confidence in the life-force had to be present, before the initial interest in improving your life began. By now you will have figured out, that you can really trust the life-force originally given to you. You will be more conscious of the tremendous energy in your center. Your breath will get deeper, reaching more often into the center of your body. You will increasingly become able to clearly sense when the energy for your actions comes out of your center. The phrase: "Tantra means to live the essence of life", now takes on a real personal significance.

As you learn to trust, your perceptions of human communication will alter. Your understanding of vibrations and their wavelengths will make clear to you the frequent emptiness of words. Confidence in your ability to correctly perceive vibrations will slowly replace your reliance on verbal language.

A long time before that revelation, the media will have become much less important; you may even perceive it as an obstacle on your path. You can now trust in your ability to sort the wheat from the chaff.

It is now safer for the ego to give way to the Self. This process might happen without having been observed by the majority of people around you. You, however, will be able to distinguish between your ego and your true Self. The resulting natural self-confidence, which engenders basic satisfaction with life, permits you to be more compassionate.

One cannot rush through such a life changing process. Allow yourself to enjoy the journey. Laugh in the midst of all these tears of relief. Appreciate what you are doing. The original life-energy in you has increased and your optimism has been strengthened. As one revives the first five virtues, self-acceptance and self-love grow. Along with them healthy self-esteem is established. Social masks become unnecessary; they may even hinder true communication.

Now you are ready to live your **willingness to surrender**.

When a person is truly willing to surrender, an "absolute" letting go happens. If you "go with the flow", the flow will find you. To surrender in a tantric way is to surrender to the universe, the greater one-ness. Having felt the unity in yourself (a microcosm) you gain knowledge about the macrocosm.[1]

Only at this level can you experience the "great union" with another microcosm. This is the so-called Maithuna: the sexually expressed union of a man and a woman in one-ness with the universe.

If only one partner has completed the process of becoming a microcosm, both lovers will get caught up in psycho-dramatic[2] interactions. Most couple-relationships thrive on these psycho-dramas, holding the partners at least in a partial symbiosis. The full Maithuna can only be achieved, if both partners have first grown to complete oneness as a microcosm.

Brought into the open, this capability - of living as a microcosm within the macrocosm - would allow us to call off all knowledge and wisdom of the past and future - without speaking or writing a word. We would only need to listen attentively to our own bodies, and properly use our brain's capacity.

The misuse and corruption of language, which keeps so many of us from true knowledge, was my reason for being so reticent, for so long, in committing thoughts to print. My near death experience rekindled the desire to live in a world where people are able to live their senses. As a child, I had a faint idea that we could live by body knowledge and wisdom alone. I had always suspected that our brain's potential, combined with our physical senses, could conquer the superficiality of languages.

It took me a long time to come back to the use of spoken languages, once I had undergone several long periods of living subtle consciousness in wordless clarity. This esoteric thinking - by way of word-free concepts - surprised me with its depth.

---

[1]   "Cosmos" is of Greek origin and means "universe" as well as "all people"
[2]   These psychodramas are connected to the past of this life, and/or former lifetimes. They are always linked to karma.

The holistic healing I have practiced in different cultures over the last 33 years has made the world's misery evident. These experiences powerfully demonstrate how human beings are suffering from physical – and societal - manifestations of ill-health originated in the absence or deformation of conscious love. These widespread energetic imbalances, if left unchecked, may completely destroy our planet. Very many of us have never felt the truth of being a "materialization of love" and were not even welcomed to earth. So now, we have to start from scratch; this may be what saves us.

Outline

Before these pages lead you into practical ideas for individual growth, a glance at the all-encompassing field of ancient Hindu Tantra is taken. This overview is unavoidable for the comprehension of the latter chapters. Kept as brief as possible, it also intends to highlight particular aspects of Tantra, over which confusion seems to reign.

Tantra is gaining renewed importance in this special era, which was foreseen by ancient Hinduism. Predicted changes for these unique times will be interpreted from the viewpoint of Central American Mayan cosmology as well.

Subsequently, we are going to examine the effects of change on a personal level. Circumstances are increasingly pressuring us into individual transformation on an almost daily basis. Thus, methods of letting go and clearing out one's personal past will be illustrated in detail. Practical exercises and meditations, developed especially for positively experienced liberation, will also be offered. These meditations have their background in historical energy knowledge; however "cosmic intercourse" derives directly from Hindu Tantra. These exercises are designed to enhance your own creativity; with practice you may discover new versions that are better suited to your needs.

The book progresses to the conscious relationship between a man and woman, with respect to the tantric bond. Statements about homosexuality, an important aspect of life in our time, are included in this section.

THEORETICAL BACKGROUND OF HINDU TANTRA

BASIC INFORMATION

TANTRA literally means "expansion". "It is that knowledge, which expands mind, body and consciousness."[3] This way of living emphasizes the essence of life and the significance of energy in general. Its focus on the unification of opposites manifests in the biological world as the union of female and male.

TANTRA,
the Union of Opposites
or the
Union of Universal Yin /Yang

The expansion into oneness, i.e. becoming a microcosm by unifying yin and yang, is above all an individual process. Having reached a balance of yin and yang in oneself, "White Tantra" can be lived. "White Tantra" is frequently called the "Grandfather of Hatha-Yoga". It was taught to male children from an early age, to enable their use of energy in the body. Female children also learned the use of energetic guidance according to their nature. Thus, in ancient India the young – usually of the higher social classes – were trained to use and send forth energy consciously.

"White Tantra" means to expand one's energy as positive vibrations. These vibrations emanate from one's energy-field. The effect of White Tantra is intensified by connecting it with positive wavelengths of thoughts and wishes.

"Black Tantra" was known as sending negatively effective vibrations to someone, doing harm.

---

[3] as described in the Kashika Vritti scriptures

"Red Tantra" means to send forth positive vibrations from the cumulative life-creating energy of the "*Maithuna*".

Tantra honors the four directions, applying them even to the human body.

upper body
north

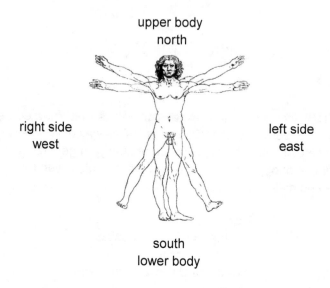

right side   left side
west   east

south
lower body

HISTORICAL BACKGROUND

The origins of Tantra can be traced back to ancient India. Relics have been found which are over 5000 years old. More than one hundred ancient texts describe the tantric system in detail.

Tantra was, and rarely still is, practiced in Hindu-temples in the form of religious rituals. In its origin the practical life of Brahmins[4] was tantric, a cosmological existence in its depth and knowledge.

3500 years ago the tantric way of life in India sprouted the first hints of deformation. About a thousand years later, in a region 300 km wide, adjoining the Ganges for 600 km, Buddha introduced the countryside to his new philosophical and theological hypothesis. Although originally some local Kings in Northern India had followed his sermons, asked for this advice and supported him, it did not take long for the population of Benares[5] to line up against Buddha's teachings. Despite the initial setbacks, his teachings eventually came to influence one of the most powerful emperors of Ancient India, Emperor Asoka. It was through Asoka's efforts, that 200 years after Buddha's death, a Synod was held in Pataligama[6]. Its purpose was to amalgamate the remaining historical texts, which now comprise Buddha's legacy. Asoka's son, Mahinda, eventually introduced Ceylon[7] to Buddhism in the third century BC.

As a new religious system, "Buddhism" mainly migrated north. After two missionary periods, spread over a 1000 years, the areas now known as Nepal and Tibet became strict centers of Buddhism.

Buddha's goal had been to avoid further decadence of the Hindu religion. Obviously too many social norms would have needed to change, therefore a reformation of Hinduism through Buddha and his convictions did not succeed.

---

4   Brahmins were - before Buddha lived - the highest of the four social classes (castes) in India
5   the former "Forest of Bliss" and then center of Brahmanism in northern India – now called Varanasi. It is considered one of the three oldest cities in the world
6   now called Patna
7   modern Sri Lanka is still strongly influenced by Buddhism

Buddhism developed its own tantric system, which seems to focus mainly on the four upper Chakras[8]. The Tibetan Shambala tradition has many similarities with Hindu Tantra, upon which this work is based. While being a profound tantric system, its boundaries far exceed those of a religious system.

There were 65 tantric arts and sciences expounded upon in the relatively late and from original Tantra quite distinct "Kama Sutra" scriptures (circa 300 A.D.), among them: Alchemy, Architecture, Astrology, Astronomy, Chemistry, Dance, Gardening, Magic, Mathematics, Medicine, Music, Palmistry, and Poetry.

The goal of Tantra was total spiritual awareness of the physical body - down to the tiniest cell. The art of sexual love was the noblest of the tantric sciences. Just as in the rest of those 65 sciences, the techniques of tantric love-expression were not an end in and of themselves. They were - and are - vehicles for growth towards enlightenment and completion. Love was carefully thought about and experienced as the life-creating force. The Tantrics knew how to use the radiation of energy and light-fullness which is the natural outcome of this force. The embodied act of love was meditative devotion, intertwining the communication of two microcosms as particles of the macrocosm. They had found a way to sanction the gift of energy reception from the universe. This sacred union led to the perception of boundless knowledge[9].

The body was considered as the "temple of the spirit" on earth. It was from this temple that one conducted oneself with family, society as a whole, the world and the universe.

---

[8]　energy centers in the body

[9]　The Mayan priest class in Meso-America apparently used similar ways to discover and explore even beyond our solar system. Like the Indian Tantrics, the Mayan priests opened up to conscious perception of the universe through sexual union.

SPECIFIC KNOWLEDGE ABOUT ENERGY

We Are Energy

Every being is animated through energy: humans, animals and plants.

The correlation of energy and matter was at the core of Tantric knowledge about the human body. Max Planck would eventually rediscover this many centuries later: "Materie ist eine Form von Energie mit unterschiedlicher Frequenz."[10]

The material energy of the body is linked to the earth. This physical body is animated by spiritual energy, which is linked to the universe. When this link to the universe is weakened, and the connection of spirit to the body is not functioning well, disease is the outcome.

Energy in general is neutral. It is never "good" or "bad", "positive" or "negative", however energy can only be applied in two ways:
➢ perceived as "positive", constructive or creative;
     it is light-full and expansive.
➢ perceived as "negative", destructive - even in creation;
     it is dark and contracting.

Where we feel heaviness in our body, the energy is contracted or blocked. The energy field (aura) around the body is darkened in the affected areas. When we feel light and joyful in our body, the energy expands and is visible in the aura as light or light-full colors.

Love is energy used in a creative - constructive way. Through its expansive and penetrating vibration, love-energy can effectively change the energy and situation of a group of people, a room, a street, - and with enough power or persistence - a world.

---

[10] "Matter is a type of energy with a variation of frequency"

Polarity and Balance

One can observe in the philosophical basis of tantric life the importance of polarity. The positive and negative poles are even represented in the original creation myth[11].

Without thinking about it, we work with polarity even during our most mundane tasks.

➢ Right-handed people use the right side as the active, giving side. The right is the positive pole (= yang = male) while the left side is the negative pole, passive and receiving (= yin = female).

➢ Left-handed people have the poles switched around.

The energy-circle is closed, when positive pole/hand and negative pole/hand are brought together. This is the original meaning of the "Namaste"-salutation in India, Nepal and Tibet: One complete energy-circle, one microcosm, greets the other microcosm.

Originally, the Chakras[12] of men and women were biologically charged to correspond. Since these energy centers have the opposite charge in the male and female, we should not be surprised about the force of biological attraction between the sexes.

Through conscious use of mindful willpower, the poles can be reversed by a person who has grown to be a microcosm, having fully balanced yin and yang.

As it pertains to polarity, the goal of Tantra is above all the perfect balance of yin and yang within the microcosm. Using the energy-channels (nadis) to guide the internal energy flow, conscious awareness of the entire body can be achieved. Of course, the external energy exchange happening within the social - and environmental - context will affect you. That's why the art of freely giving and receiving needs to be developed - and requires full awareness.

Obviously, with this background, the equality of male and female partners was never an issue in true Tantra.

---

[11]   Union of Shakti and Shiva
[12]   see page 10

Yin/Yang in a person
(ancient version)

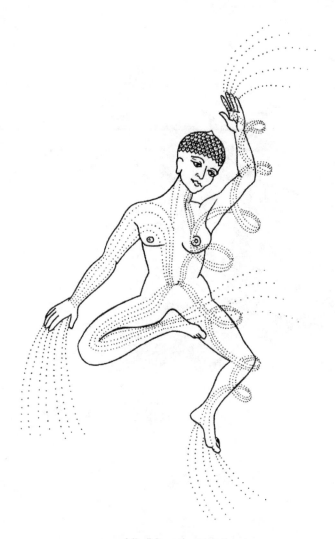

Yin/Yang in a person
(version of our era
considering
the flow of energy)

The Body's Energy-Field, Energy-Centers and Energy-Channels

Tantric masters have discerned five oscillating layers of the body, which are interconnected to form the energy-field/aura. These layers vibrate at the same frequency when a person is healthy. In instances of disease, stress, or life changes, the frequency rate of the layers differ.

The outer layer forms the materiality of the physical body. The second layer denotes respiration. The third layer is cognition or the cognitive field. The fourth layer is the "emotional body". The fifth and innermost layer is formed by the Chakra system. This innermost layer is called the *brahma-nadi*, and as it permeates upwards and outwards across the other layers, it is used to tap into the energy of the universe.

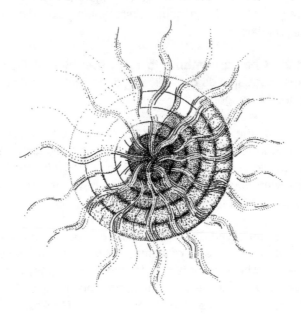

The five oscillating layers

The Chakra system is the body's intuitive, or psychic energy system, through which one may achieve physical ecstasy and spiritual unity. Through subtle energy-channels, called "nadis", the Chakras are connected to one or more of the other four layers, thus energetically nourishing the whole body. A number of nadis are similar to the meridians of the acupuncture-system, as well as the biological nervous system. By use of mind-power however, any nadi can be imagined, formed and put to use.[13] The three main nadis in the body are *susumna* within the spine, with *ida* and *pingala* running closely along the spine, on the left and right side respectively.

Chakras are often referred to as "disks" or "wheels". You will probably find some confusing information about the chakra system. By and large, seven Chakras are known to exist in the human body[14]:

1st Chakra: a.k.a. the "Base Chakra", "Ground Chakra", "Root Chakra", "Pelvic Plexus", in Sanskrit: *Muladhara* (*mula* = root, cause, source; *adhara* = support or vital part). It's located at the coccyx or tale-bone.

2nd Chakra: a.k.a. the "Sexual Chakra", "Hypogastric Plexus", in Sanskrit: *Svadhisthana* (*sva* = vital force, soul, *adhisthana* = seat of, or abode). It's located at the genitals.

The 1st and 2nd Chakra combine to form the "Sacral Plexus". This "Sacral Plexus" corresponds dynamically to the materialization of life on Earth; facilitated by the genitals.

3rd Chakra: a.k.a. the "Central Chakra", "Cosmic Center", in Sanskrit: *Manipuraka.* The word *Manipura* (navel) points out its location at the navel, which is the cosmic center of the human body. It includes the "Hara" - or earth center - lying about one inch below the navel. It also corresponds energetically to the abdominal organs.

4th Chakra: a.k.a. the "Heart Chakra", "Cardiac Plexus", in Sanskrit: *Anahata Chakra* (*anahata* = heart), "seat of intimacy". Located at the bottom of the sternum, it resides where the nerves sympaticus and parasympaticus form the only nerve center, which is not in the brain. The vitality of the heart and circulatory system depends on the condition of this Chakra.

---

[13] The female body has 84 000 nadis, the male body has 72 000 nadies
[14] Reports of esoteric knowledge, being divulged in Mexico, describe seven planetary Chakras:
Three Mountain-Chakras: Mexico, Peru, Tibet
Three Dessert-Chakras: Mongolia, Sahara, Sumeria and
One Neutral Chakra: Europe

The 3rd and 4th Chakra combine to form the "Solar Plexus".

5th Chakra: a.k.a. the "Throat Chakra", "Carotid Plexus", in Sanskrit: *Visuddha Chakra* (*visuddha* = pure). It is linked to the thyroid, parathyroid and thymus glands.

6th Chakra: a.k.a. the "Third Eye", in Sanskrit: *Ajna Chakra* (*ajna* = command). Between the two eyebrows, a horizontal line can be drawn from it through the pituitary and onwards to the pineal gland in the brain.

7th Chakra: a.k.a. the "Crown Chakra", in Sanskrit: *Sahasrara Chakra* or *Brahma Randhra* (*sahasrara* = thousand petalled lotus, *brahma* = absolute, universe): located on the scalp, at a point where the spine, if extended, would meet the top of the head. Its vertical linkage to the pineal gland has a physical purpose that is not yet clear to Western medicine.

The **6th and 7th Chakra,** can be connected through a visualized 90-degree angle. The base of this right angle would lead horizontally from the Third Eye to the pineal gland and then upwards to the Crown Chakra. Therefore, the pineal is pivotal to the reception of supreme energy.

The seven Chakras

There are many depictions of Chakras, in which the author claims that each of them has a specified color and/or form. Studying quite a lot of East-Indian literature on Tantra and Chakras, I have not found any information regarding a general connection of one certain color with each Chakra except for the Heart Chakra. According to the ancient Indian knowledge it is connected with red color while the Heart Chakra itself is considered as the real heart. Our present perception has come to the knowledge that the colors of our auras and Chakras vary according to particular emotions, and since these feelings are wide-ranging, it is not possible to depict Chakras with fixed attributes. Our feelings overlap, this ever-changing mixture becomes evident in the momentary color combinations of our Chakras and auras. The color red is for instance often connected with aggression (Latin "agredere" = "going towards the world"), green with harmony, etc.

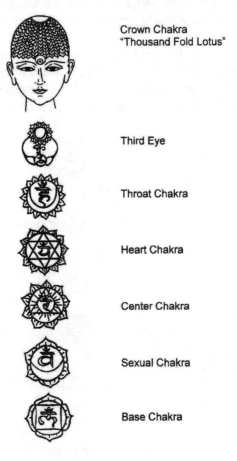

Crown Chakra
"Thousand Fold Lotus"

Third Eye

Throat Chakra

Heart Chakra

Center Chakra

Sexual Chakra

Base Chakra

The Yantras of all Chakras

A Yantra was[15] used in tantric symbolism in order to visualize an individual Chakra. The Chakras were also sounded out using corresponding mantric expressions. These mantras are inscribed in Sanskrit at the center of each of the first five Yantras. It is interesting to note that the old masters did not try to ascribe worldly lettering to the two chakras, which are connected to the universe[16].

Through mind- and willpower we can enhance the natural flow of energy through the nadis, as their course clearly connects the Chakras. In Tantra, energy is consciously channeled from the lower Chakras into the higher ones and vice versa. Incorporating this into daily practice, one has no choice but to integrate refined moral and ethical values. Through this increased channeling the physical body can achieve a unification of earth and universal energy within. With this insight into cosmic wisdom, one can begin to grasp the full memory, as well as significance, of former lifetimes.

Kundalini

The "Panchastavi", a hymn of praise exalting Kundalini - the Cosmic Life-Energy, describes it as an "Instrument of Liberation". The Panchastavi was found hidden in a high mountain cave in Kashmir. This enchanting hymn contemplates on Kundalini as a medium for the achievement of inner illumination.

A radiant flow of energy arising from the Root Chakra, Kundalini streams upwards, intersecting the spine at each Chakra disc, until it reaches the Crown Chakra. It can create a "revolution in the brain". This "Serpent Power" coursing along the spine, is sensed as a "Wave of Bliss" or "Wave of Beauty" as it pulses through the Chakras, finally invigorating the nerve centers in the brain.

Kundalini arousal was a distinctive feature of the Brahmins, the spiritual hierarchy and therefore ruling class, of ancient India. According to their name, the Brahmins were supposed to be connected with Brahma, the Absolute Consciousness, the Universe, hence the main energy-channel of our body, located in the spine is also called the Brahma-Nadi. Once Kundalini has arisen, the physical position of the coccyx changes. Some of

---

[15] Traditional Hindu devotees have retained this practice up until today.
[16] see Beej Mantras, page 22

today's Brahmins are still cultivating this seed of knowledge, even though getting to this advanced stage is also a rarity for them[17].

Dormant in all of us, Kundalini cannot be awakened merely through certain practices of Hatha-Yoga, or Pranayama[18]. There was even a specific discipline developed - from the original yoga disciplines - for this end, yet many professional teachers of Kundalini-Yoga are on a meandering path. This doesn't mean that their students are necessarily precluded from awakening their blissful Serpent Power. During the practice of pranayama or certain asanas[19], startling sensations may come up in the Kundalini-area of the body[20]. Enjoyable tickling, itching or erotic sensations - may begin surging up the spine: causing flashes of light, or the perception of lightening, in the brain. Unfortunately, this is not a sure sign, that Kundalini-power has been embodied.

Kundalini-power is only vigorous after consciousness transformation has created a hybrid form of spiritual energy that has merged with the nervous system of the entire body. Modern science is still in the dark about this hybrid energy, which enables the flow of "reproductive secretions" into different internal organs, including the brain. This subtle nectar, amrita, is described on page 72.

The life long pursuit of tedious exercises and esoteric disciplines, which were often dangerous or painful, has never assured illumination. The awakening of Kundalini-power is a goal that cannot be met by wishful thinking, which only serves to enlarge the ego with ideas of self-importance. The enlargement of the ego and the build-up of self-importance are like a one-dimensional "overview", wherein the drop of water is considered more important than the ocean. One must be willing to surrender to the "tide of the universe".

Signs of awakened Kundalini-power are not easy to recognize by the naked eye: inner illumination, abounding love, humility, conscious thought-forms and diction - all this inspired by an altered perception of the "objective" world. A radical experience of the Kundalini-power transcends

---

[17]   Information gleamed from personal talks with Brahmins in Varanasi, Oct. 1995
[18]   *prana* = breath of life, essence of life; *yama* = concentrate on, embrace; pranayama = science of breath
[19]   asana = yoga posture
[20]   below the navel down to the perineum, called *kanda*.

every concept of philosophy and religion, even the Hindu religion, where all this knowledge has its origin.

According to the Panchastavi, Kundalini is the everyday experience of the accomplished yogi or yogini. "What the ego of the illuminated person perceives is a Splendor, sublime beyond description, dwelling in the body, still prone to hunger, thirst, sleep, fatigue, desire and passion, in a rational way but, at the same time, conscious of its own eternal substance, as if the sun had bodily descended to live in and illuminate a narrow, dark and dingy cavern on earth."[21]

"Shakti" corresponds to "Kundalini", personalized in other ancient literature she is called "Savitri", the spouse of Brahma – the Absolute or Creator. On earth, in men, Brahma is the still unconscious "Satiavan". He is the "Son of the Sun", whereas Savitri is the "Daughter of the Universe". In the Hymn to Sativer from the RigVeda[22], Savitri is called "Sayitri"[23]. She is the Goddess of Light named "Vidmata", which literally means the mother of the Vedic scriptures. Therefore, one can easily conclude that Kundalini itself, the cosmic life-force in the human body, brought forth the ancient scriptures of India.

A cursory exploration of most ancient cultures would reveal a series of descriptive myths, all intended to inform about the enlightenment available through Kundalini. In the Central American culture of the Maya, the Serpent Power is awakened by a kiss from "Sak Nikte", Princess of the Life-power. In the Assyro-Babylonian culture, Kundalini is personified in Ishtar, the wife of the Sun-God and God of Fertility: "Tammuz". In Asia Minor "Cybele" was known as the Power of Life, the Goddess of Fertility and Creation. A later derivation in the Eastern Mediterranean culture, "Medusa", had an abundance of Kundalini as her head was full of serpents. Minerva, Isis, Frya, the list could be endless.

The mythic lore could give one the impression that Kundalini-power is only available to women. This cosmic life force is in everyone, the higher Reality doesn't distinguish between the sexes.

---

[21] Gopi Krishna: Ancient Secrets of Kundalini, page 129
[22] The RigVeda is one of the entire Vedas, which are the Sacred Scriptures of the Hindus, "Veda" means literaly "wisdom", "knowledge of the heard", "revealed"
[23] Gopi Krishna, page 129

The biological factors - human sexuality - responsible for mystical ecstasy, entitle us with the original ability to float in the "ocean of the universe". If we try to ignore that fact, the "Cosmic Reservoir" of Kundalini will remain untapped. The mystical experience (samadhi) influences our brethren like a drop of water falling in the pond of humanity, with the ripples flowing outwards to the social ocean.

Having sourced this cosmic life-energy, a person discovers the internal dance of joy. They become cognizant of whatever happens around them, taking on the social roles they need to, as they move around the earth at will. Such a person knows that the invisible Kundalini is the embodied spirit, hidden by Maya - the veil of illusion.

There is no way, "to make curious crowds their partner in the secret"[24], like Gopi Krishna points out so well. Even spiritual intellectuals, well versed in the world of words concerning cosmic know how, are not able to budge the handle of the door, which opens the "room of light-fullness". The Persian poet and mystic Rumi wrote cynically: "Like an ass laden with books, heavy is the knowledge that is not inspired by 'Him'".[25]

If one has a craving for it, or even attempts to purchase it, the "Power Reservoir of Kundalini" is simply drained away. The logical result of that attitude is to live "spiritual materialism", while persuading yourself that you are following the true path. Liberation is only possible by actually living one's Self-identity, in tandem with Brahma, the Absolute, - free of material fears and clinging, without attachment to one's personal history.[26] "Men who have no riches, who live on recognized food, who have perceived the 'Void' and 'Unconditional Freedom' (= nirvana), their path is difficult to understand, like that of birds in the air".[27]

This liberation leads to a state of crystalline clarity in both mind and body, a Cosmic Intelligence, feeling the Spirit vibrantly in every cell. According to Vedic philosophy, the doctrine of Cosmic Intelligence forms the basis of Tantra's traditions.

---

[24] Gopi Krishna: page 51
[25] Nicolson Reynole A.: Rumi – Poet and Mystic, Allen and Unwin, London, page 76
[26] see the scriptures of "Shankaracharya", quoted from Gopi Krishna, page 36
[27] attibuted to Buddha's scriptures of "Dhammapada" see Gopi Krishna, page 36

According to the teachings, a way of life as the Ultimate Being[28], along with raised Kundalini, liberates the spirit walking on earth (âtman) from the Samsara. This cycle of reincarnations is completed when one has fully converted Karma into Dharma[29]. The decision to return, after the last material death, is now taken free from compulsion.

The base of my spine, or coccys, started its substantial shift in 1988 while I was high up in the region of Cusco and Machu Picchu, surviving a five-month Peruvian winter. Indeed, the most significant day for this shift was the summer solstice as celebrated in North America.

During my first sojourn at the ruins of Machu Picchu a subtle urge drove me to make the long trek up to Huaynapicchu. Something, not someone, at the top of this mountain was waving to me.

On the way, other wanderers gave me plenty of strange looks, probably because I almost danced the terrain bare-foot while they trudged along in heavy hiking boots. Like always, at ruins or naturally occurring places of high energy, I remained bare-foot, thereby allowing the energy to flow; unobstructed by any footwear.

Having reached the summit of Huaynapicchu, the impulse to lie down at certain spots was clear. Stretched out there, in the position that Leonardo da Vinci made famous in his circle drawing, I felt myself being woven into the fabric of the universe. I have been using this spread-eagled position to connect since 1979, when, while reclining in this position on a Greek island, I had my initial embrace with the universe.

An eternity of hours later and full of energy, I scampered back down to Machu Picchu's ruins. There feeling the vastness of the lawn, while once more in the "Leonardo-da-Vinci-position"[30], I opened all my Chakras towards the earth and universe. I sensed a strong shift at the root of my spine, from that moment my coccyx was straightened out and it stayed that way for over fourteen months. I still had no idea why this was happening.

Back in Mexico on the last evening of the same year, I met David in San Cristobal. This tall Mexican of obvious Aztec descent and I were magnetized by the unusually strong attraction that vibrated between us. We had a strong connection from our last reincarnation in WW II in Germany.

---

[28] microcosm
[29] karma = "binding knots of action or reaction"
      dharma = "supreme occupation"
[30] see illustration on page 2

The ensuing sexual relationship released unsuspected energy from my sacral plexus. It shot up through, and along, my spine in a snake-like movement to my brain where it exploded into a storm of lightening. The relief, which had spread through my spine, back and 7th Chakra, brought my entire body into harmonic convergence.

A couple of months later, on the very day of my brother's arrival in Mexico for a vacation, I was almost unable to get up from my bed. This semi-paralysis persisted for the next week as my coccyx shifted again. Years later, the Brahmins helped me decipher the significance of this shift.

ORIGINAL TANTRIC
TERMINOLOGY AND SYMBOLISM

In the old tantric way of life, physical senses were trained with full consciousness. It was recognized that the physical senses needed to be awakened and enhanced for one to live life's full potential.

Yantras served to stimulate energy and its movement through visualizations.
A number of Yantras are geometrically precise drawings with colored symbols, depicting different goddesses, which were at the core one: Shakti. Besides these Shakta-Yantras of the Goddesses, there were also Architectural Yantras (ground plans for temples), Astrological Yantras, Numerical Yantras and the previously mentioned Chakra Yantras.

The most dynamic Shakta-Yantra, illustrated on the following pages, is the Shri Yantra. It represents the "most beautiful and ever-young graceful goddess", Tripurasundari. She symbolizes the "Desire Principle of the Supreme", and is the Mother of the Gods Shiva, Vishnu and Brahma.

The bindu at the center of this Yantra exemplifies the true Self, the spirit as cosmic energy in the human being. Since the microcosm is a mirror of the macrocosm, this bindu represents individual cosmic consciousness. The inner circle delineates a balanced microcosm through the intertwined female and male triangles.[31] The twin circle of petals, which in themselves represent the moon, entwine the giving and receiving from the micro to the macrocosm. The social component of this universal exchange is portrayed on the perimeter by the four directions.

Mantras stimulated energy through sound. Although numerous Mantras were chanted, they were composed of only one, or a very few meaningful Sanskrit words. Used soundly, the multiple repetitions tuned the devotee to a high spiritual and physical wavelength. The deepening "enchantment" allowed the Center Chakra to be brought into focus, thus providing a source of power for progressively finer tuning.

---

[31] The female triangle points downwards, whereas the male triangle points upwards

Sri Yantra

Geometrical structure
of the Sri Yantra

"OM" was, and still is, considered as the "best, first and last Mantra". As "OM" is the short form for "AUM", it can be deconstructed as follows:

➤ "A" > *sattva* > the Creator the waking state, absolute consciousness. It symbolizes God Brahma.

➤ "U" > *rajas* > the Preserver the dream state, inner consciousness of subjective thoughts, feelings and desires. It symbolizes God Vishnu.

➤ "M" > *tamas* > the Destroyer the state of deep sleep, the consciousness of complete but unaware unity. It symbolizes God Shiva.

While chanting, one can meditate on "AUM", picturing the philosophical interpretation of the lotus-blossom, which grows from the unconsciousness "M" (mud) through the subconscious "U" (water) and into the visibility of open consciousness "A" (air).

The Mantra "OM" or "AUM" should be sounded out in a deep tone, the "A" or "O" stimulating the Center Chakra. Before starting out with the Mantra, the decision needs to be made as to whether OM or AUM will be chanted. There is a slight, but significant difference: OM rises faster from the 3rd Chakra into the brain, whereas AUM ascends more evenly through the Heart and Throat Chakras. Finally, the M reverberates, similar to the buzzing of a bee, at the top of the cranium. As the Mantric resonance uncorks the cerebral cortex, it frees stored convulsions and repressions. It restores the brain's innate capacity for the integration of new concepts and intuitive creations.

The specific Mantras for the Chakras are visually articulated with a Sanskrit letter in the centers of the ancient Yantras, except for those of the two higher Chakras. There is actually no word meaning for any of these *Beej Mantras*. There is no intellectual concept of the *Beej Mantras*, only frequent and long-term chanting of these Mantras can lead to a deeper knowing, empowered by the physical vibration in the body. Practicing the Beej Mantras activates the Chakras and the energy circulation between them[32].

Mudras profoundly influenced the body's energy through touch and tactile sense. Mudras were finger and hand gestures, as well as body postures, through which aspects of the higher Reality were symbolized.

---

[32]   also see Inner Flute, page 65

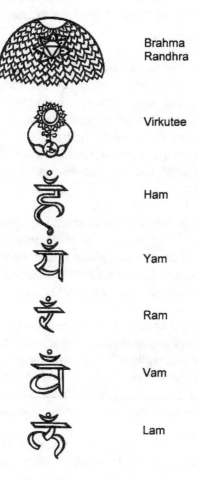

Brahma
Randhra

Virkutee

Ham

Yam

Ram

Vam

Lam

Beej Mantras
of the Chakras

Nyasas were the combination of yantric visualizations, mantric sounds and the conscious touching of the Mudras - applied with the true inner motion - to purify balance, and elevate the oscillation of the Chakras.

Shaktipats are performed by some spiritual teachers in parts of the West. Purported to be Nyasas, they are focused on the Third Eye of the initiate.

Hatha-Yoga traces its origins from *ha* (sun) and *tha* (moon). *Hatha* expresses the sun/moon interplay, or the yang/yin connection. *Yoga* means "union", "communion", coming from the Sanskrit term *yui* (join, or to put ones concentration on). Originally it was created as a discipline for male children as a part of "White Tantra".[33] Girls were similarly trained for flexibility of movement, in a way suited to their body's nature. The body's agility was an integral part of the conscious "programming" of the Brahmin cast in old India.

Pranayama is the science of breath. In its complex meaning *prana* stands for "breath", "respiration", "vitality", "wind", "energy" and "strength". The word *prana* is an absolute plural, indicating vital breath - the life force itself. *Yama* means to concentrate on, embrace. "Ayama" means "length", "expansion", "stretching" and "restraint".

Pranayama is of special importance in the art of conscious loving. This extension of breath and its rhythmic control is necessary for the conscious transmission of energy to the partner. Retaining or holding the breath fortifies both the physique and the anima. A proper rhythmic pattern, of slow but deep breathing, may set the mind free to enhance concentration and ecstasy. The ultimate objective of pranayama is to arouse Kundalini.

Swara Yoga, the science of the nostrils, is relevant to the respiratory nadis *pingala* and *ida*, which undulate down to the base of the spine[34]. *Pingala*, as the nadi of the sun, starts from the right nostril; *ida*, the nadi of the moon, from the left nostril. Both correspond to the opposite side of the brain. Running between these two nadis is the "Nadi of the Fire", *susumna (also called Brahma Nadi)*, which is the main channel for the flow of nerve energy inside the spinal column. The Chakras are an energy concentration which encompasses *pingala*, *ida* and *susumna*.

---

[33]   see page 1
[34]   1st Chakra

Besides the sun and moon, the nostrils and nadis correspond to specific planets in our solar system. Half an hour before sunrise, in accordance with the ruling planet of the day, the corresponding nostril takes over the inhalation.

The intricate science of Swara Yoga, may be even more enigmatic for Westerners than Pranayama, since a hectic lifestyle does not promote conscious breathing. Many people do at times inhale intensely, but only when smoking.

Terms for the Sexual Organs:

The Hindu scriptures about the art of love were partially written as a dialog between Shakti and Shiva. There were quite a number of poetic words to describe the sexual organs:

Female   Male

for the vagina: for the penis:
   - yoni   - lingam
   - shakti   - wand of light
   - sacred space   - jade stalk
   - golden doorway   - scepter of light
   - flower heart   - healing scepter
   - precious gateway   - god's organ
   - gateway to heaven
   - pleasure field of heaven
   - cave of light-fullness

for the clitoris:
   - jewel
   - bell

THE SIGNIFICANCE OF
TANTRA IN OUR ERA

Ancient books of Hindu Tantra refer to our times as the

Age of Darkness (*Kali Yuga*).

Kali Yuga is the age, "when society reaches a stage, where property confers rank,
wealth becomes the only source of virtue...
falsehood the source of success in life...
and when outer trappings are confused with inner religions".[35] [36]

Human beings are often conceived in confusion, and seem to grow up in even more turmoil. They have to deal with a double set of fears: the primal fear of being a naked animal on earth and the fear caused by the social commotion they cannot escape. They internalize the manipulations of their childhood just to comply with the natural need for basic acceptance. Convinced that these social transactions are the truth, they, in turn participate in the spawning of perpetually more manipulations. This double-edged sword of fear cuts through the healthy bonds of love. Unabated, these fears serve to manipulate us to such an extent, that instead of loving - people possess their partners, family-members and friends. To superficially diminish the fear, one also seeks to gather and possess ever-increasing material goods. Instead of sustaining our existence in a balanced way, we have fallen into the trap of wasting our planet's resources in the quest for profit, implanting even more fear.

The repression of the natural persona has gone so far, that most people can no longer perceive or discern their true feelings. They are continuously thriving for new things and events outside of themselves. Only the strongest of spirits on earth have been able to avoid getting caught in this spinning wheel of destruction. Interestingly enough, for the last 20 or 25

---

[35] In Vedic Scriptures, see Charles and Caroline Muir: Tantra, The Art of Conscious Loving, Page 5

[36] The entire East Indian system of the Ages is much more complex than here briefly presented.

years and in all parts of the world, many newborns have come "equipped" with a very strong spirit. They would seem to be among the broad avant-garde, helping us shift into the age, old tantric books refer to as the

Age of Truth (*Satya Yuga*)

This Age of Truth corresponds to the "5th World" or "5th Sun" of Mexican esotericism, based on the cosmology of ancient tribes.[37]

The *Satya Yuga* characterizes a humane world, where the truth of each spirit is lived. Actions always emerge authentically from a person's own center, the spirit, which is grounded and has clear purpose. These veritable humans interact with the world outside of themselves, represented by the four cardinal points.

In this world, the free will of a person is not cut down in childhood like in the Age of Darkness, or 4th World. The child is respected as a complete and knowledgeable spirit, although unaware of its knowledge. The capacities, the child arrives with, merely unfold in the new social field, wherein the infant only needs to learn how to deal with the new physical materiality. The main emotion of such a consciously conceived child is self-confidence; this is in sharp contrast to the constant fear a child feels in the Age of Darkness. Human lives are often felled like so many trees to please others and the society in the 4th World[38], whereas the 5th World allows for full maturity.

In our present period of change we need to distinguish
- our conditioning from our nature and
- our judgments, which are results of our conditioning, from our real wants and needs.

In the transition to the Age of Truth, there is a bidding to uncover the senses needed to perceive our own true nature. Our real feelings - not the feelings, we were trained to have - must be revealed. This can only be done through our own efforts. Our real feelings are our truth. We are on earth as spirits for no other reason than to live our truth, and to express

---

[37] For reasons of the change into the "5th World", the old Maya calendar which finished 2012, overlaps with a new calendar based on "Mayanism", which started on July 26, 1995, created by Jose Argüelles. The description of the shift from the 4th to the 5th Sun is originally handed down from the Aztecs.

[38] In Mexico's towns, full grown trees get trimmed to the point of depicting animals or birds.

ourselves according to it. Restrictive social habits may cause shyness and unease about speaking the truth of our spirit at the outset. In spite of this, the awareness gained by "going for it" will reap rewards.

This current urge for harmonization and unification of energy is apparent in individuals, as well as the entire human race. It is a result of an energy shift in the universe, where light and darkness continuously balance and harmonize. Occurring over eons, these incomprehensible and fundamental shifts are the only constant in the universe. In this cosmic period, planet earth is playing an important role in the process, widely explained and celebrated in terms of "Harmonic Convergence" since 1987.

During this change - from the Age of the Darkness to the Age of the Truth - we are being called to release our energy. Rooted in long-standing energy blocks, unheeded illness now starts to manifest in many ways. These circumstances are physically urging us to live spirit and its energy truthfully.

In this transition period our organisms need to release energy; whether our mind-set, trained through religion and/or society, allows this release or tries to hinder it. The most profound energy-discharge happens through an orgasm, which has intense healing power. However, forcing oneself, or another person, into any kind of energy-release can just block the energy anew.

Judgments, especially pre-judgments or prejudices, set you against your own truth and the truth of others. Values must evolve and broaden: things are no longer "supposed to be", nothing "has to be", "should" be or "must" be. The key to this change is being equally considerate of the Self and the Other, being aware of this equality in every action. Egotism, and its cousin altruism, can no longer bear the weight of their own imbalance. There is a cosmic thrust towards the equilibrium of the "I" and You"; with every-one living a clear natural egoism, sustaining the physical body, the spirit's temple.

As the universe/macrocosm, originates in the yin/yang pair of opposites, the microcosm also contains these contrary forces. Nevertheless, the masculine yang and the feminine yin are not expressed as such in the higher Reality. The teachings of ancient Tantra consider the highest union of cosmic consciousness as the union of Shakti and Shiva[39]. This union (which modern science has tried to describe as a huge explosion) is the force that created the universe. Shakti as the dynamic power, and Shaktiman / Shiva as the static force, are still active in the continuing shifts and changes of this original creation.

In old agricultural societies, husband and wife, whether willing or not, formed a single microcosm. Each partner understood him or herself as being half of the One. When the "other half" died, there wasn't that much desperation. The economic and nurturing system of the family cared for them, and their participation in the social system remained meaningful. Advanced spirits have always lived as a microcosm even in such societies, although often alone. This union of yin and yang in oneself is the basic premise of a tantric relationship. Brahmin couples, practicing high Tantra, were never directly involved in farming activities.

The first big step in this change from Darkness to Truth has to be taken individually, with the knowledge that the power to affect change lies only in, and for oneself. Each one of us must let go of the past! It is no coincidence, that the 20th century brought us psychology, psychoanalyses, all manner of psycho-therapies and sociology as new human sciences.

Today it may seem like tribal factions, nation states, and conglomerates are gaining power as never before. This apparent trend will only hasten its own demise, because these power grabs are so blatant that the rest of us are being pushed to react by awakening our consciousness. Some of us may try to hold on to past atrocities, but - as the very few decidedly let go - the many are nudged into awareness. By simple example, these few individuals will send tremors throughout the social and political structures, which will end the world as we know it.

"Money makes the world go round" but as the Age of Truth dawns, energy in the form of money regains the original rendition of *Arth*. This Sanskrit word delineates "money" as well as the "meaning of action". Deeds committed in the earning of money, even for basic survival, will progressively achieve full accord with your personal path. The satisfaction of sustaining yourself well through the gifting of your talents, is a major development on the road to perceiving life as a materialization of love. By

---

[39] Shiva is the God of Destruction (and Dance), who also destroys destruction. He forms part of a trinity with Brahma and Vishnu (see page 22).

going through this fundamental shift, we will eventually arrive in a joyful garden. We will be light-full and walk our paths with an aptitude for the complete use of energy.

Relationships today are often outwardly on the road to ruin. Prominent for their chaos, they are actually on the fast track from the old "half of a unity" mode to a "unity of yin and yang" in each partner. No one knows our vulnerabilities better than those with whom we share our deepest feelings. In the conflict between partners, the pain, caused by well-aimed seeds of observation, can ripen into a most beneficial harvest of catharsis. Until now, few of us have realized how important the pain of relationship is in the process of Self-discovery. The inherent social/global upheaval is closely bound to the inner changes, so many of us are now enduring.

Inner changes in so many, lead to outer changes, causing still deeper inner changes. It is not just the planet that goes through tremendous shifts. We humans go through mental and psychological "earthquakes" in the same manner.

Former union
of a couple

Union of two microcosms
(notice the inherent
symbol of infinity)

Shift of yin and yang in couples

The universal union allows each of the partners openness towards other people and also intimacy with them.

BECOMING A MICROCOSM: THE PERSONAL PATH

FEELING THE CHANGE IN ONESELF

The word "all" magnified, encompasses the entire universe or cosmos.

"Alone" means "all one". All, that I am, do, feel and think is one within me - me being part of the Greater One.

"Lonely" is missing the "all". This lack of "all" describes the missing completeness, fullness. A sense of connection with the Greater One is not felt.

To be or to become a microcosm, you are simply alone. You are living or searching for your own authentic identity, that can be only **you**. None can ever be like you.

Frequently, at the beginning of your personal growth you might feel lonely. Awful loneliness may even overcome you in a large group of people.

It's no wonder that loneliness is rampant during this final phase of the Age of Darkness. Since distrust, falseness, disharmony and confusion surround us, we often get contaminated and carry on with disharmony in ourselves. We feel dark, our hearts are not pure, and we despair of ever finding a way out.

At any given moment, something or someone might affect us heavily. Reacting in a contaminated and contagious way, we proceed to recreate further frustrations of love - hate and pain. We might feel a gnawing urge not to take part in these common social games, but most of us don't know how to interrupt this vicious cycle of destructiveness. Attempts at transforming this cycle into constructive behavior usually leave us with feelings of helplessness.

The conscious decision to leave behind this cycle involves surrendering to the unknown. Unaware of the fear this creates, we let a underlying resistance nurture the perception that we never have enough time or space for conscious decision making. We might procrastinate until a severe illness pushes us over the edge and into the unknown. We might even need a traumatic break-up to force us to live at odds with our regular routine.

See yourself in this predicament like an infant making its first insecure steps, frequently losing balance and stumbling. Without curiosity and willpower, no child could ever learn to walk. Embrace yourself, and especially your fearful inner child, with love. This is extremely important, since your inner child's fear could hinder curiosity and willpower. Be caring and loving. Take your inner child by the hand and show her or him the way: a way of beauty and joy. Find out what your inner child likes to play with, along your path of self-discovery. When difficulty, pain or even sickness show up right in the middle of your path, don't try to get rid of them by hurling judgments at them, yourself or other people. Those very same verdicts will boomerang right back. Instead, seek to unveil the intrinsic value of those difficulties and the chance they are offering you - a chance to expand your horizons. Later, you will be able to deal with similar circumstances quite differently.

Nothing in life is independent of the vibrations around it. If you find yourself suddenly dealing with a bout of loneliness, don't start thinking that there is something wrong with you again. Personal change causes shifts in your vibrational patterns, possibly your frequency will go to a new wavelength. Some people close to you might not understand, what's going on. They may respond negatively to your vibrational repositioning, which now corresponds more closely to your word-expressions and actions. Your conduct, now in sync with your purpose, might force some to reject you - leaving your social field forever. Others will be thrilled. You will attract new people, later even most likely the kind of people you also once feared.

As this metamorphosis refines your power of perception, little by little you start to plug into a telepathic internet. You will communicate with the collective unconscious and conscious of people who are on a parallel path spiritually. You will be able to upload and download from this "connectedness", an encouraging prospect.

And faster than you ever would have thought possible, you have already vaulted over a deep canyon. The "quickening" in our era pushes you ahead. Absurd situations in daily life have a whirlwind effect. Everything moves fast.

For a while, the inclination to previous stability can predominate. Too many uncertainties have manifested. Long-standing friendships, torn asunder through basic misunderstandings, may bring about overwhelming pain and longing for the old human bonds.

In the meantime, you've slipped into the use of a totally different language, without having in any way given up your mother tongue. Your conversations now emanate with vibrations that you send out and resonate with.

Understanding yourself will get hard at times. Hiding your own situation inside you might find yourself interacting much more than ever before with people on platforms of social media. A "poor me" syndrome may search for ways to dissolve the dilemma by seeking help from a friendly ear. You might seek confirmation of your path or emotional relief by opening up to someone.

When others do the same with you in trying to deal with their conflicts, now, it just might be too much for you. Not wanting to hear about it, you may try to steer clear and be aloof. On the other hand having gone through a similar situation, for which you found a positive solution, helping your fellow traveler will convey a sense of contentment.

On your path of change, you'll discover that you are suffering from situations and emotions, which form repetitive patterns and likely reach back into your early childhood. Your past and present suffering is physically stored. Pain points or disease highlight the motivation to continue anew on your path and unload the burdens you've carried for so long. Positive life experiences help to heal these acute manifestations in your body. Realizing this, you will feel the necessity to rid yourself thoroughly of thought patterns, which instigate needless conflict.

CLEARING OUT THE PAST

There is a part of you, an integral part of you, that agreed to be born in the time and place you were. Somehow you know that your family "set-up", as odious as it may have been for some, was important to your soul. Family and school gave you your first bearings for the more general instruction and orientation that would follow in this lifetime. Although most of us cannot remember the decision, our spirits also chose the town and country where all this would take place. This is the reason, sometimes subconscious, that there has always been so much in your life that you accept and deeply care for. Some of your fondest memories may even be of childhood rebellion, which was made necessary by these circumstances.

Keep this in mind, when you scrutinize your present values and priorities. It is common to come across situations in your childhood, perceived as especially negative, which formed the experiential base for what now are your most positive attributes.

Expanding your horizons to new social fields - and unfamiliar cultures - gives you a backdrop from which you can reflect upon the entire journey of your spirit. You might have a big awakening one day, when you notice that fears you always thought of as being your own were actually "hand me downs". They were the fears of your mother, father, or even culture that you just put on and wore automatically. An innate fear of snakes for instance, might be full blown in someone who has never even seen a snake. This analogy works extremely well when pondering racism and prejudice. Both are fear based, and definitely handed down through generations.

Did you ever contemplate on the imperative to adapt socially, and its power to instill fear? Children want to please their parents or caregivers; they are totally dependent upon them for survival. In addition, psychological survival demands from children that they audition hard for their respective roles in the family-psychodrama. We all had to rehearse daily for the family program. Essential dependency compelled us to heed the limits and boundaries of our parents and siblings.

If we would not have learned - even by unhealthy methods - to respect the boundaries of others, we could only stumble through life dazed and helpless, unable to cope with the world.

Once honestly considered from this point of view, all the pain we had to undergo during our socialization process doesn't feel as cumbersome.

It's obvious, that our parents were and are just individuals; with dreams, desires, frustrations, capacities and limitations. They were hurt themselves during their childhood programming process; often they felt it more profoundly and longer than we did.

During a moment of rekindled rage, stemming from our childhood or adolescence, we may be tempted to harshly judge our parents. This will not free us. With introspection, some might notice that smoldering anger is a favorite emotion. For many of us, this anger is rooted in the stump of frustration. This stump is the only surviving element of our spiritual tree, after our blossoming free will has been chopped down so effectively in the past. Expressions of our will may have been cut short so frequently in childhood that we became convinced that it "always" happened. On the other hand we might have "never" gotten, what we always wanted. All generalizations are usually caused by blinded perception. Hence the importance of proof reading your thoughts and sifting out your true emotions!

Allow this stump to sprout forth and grow to the heavens!

If need be - plant the seedling elsewhere!

You can create a ritual around the planting of a tree, caring for it, while observing it as a living symbol of your own growth and your authentic identity.

Love is stronger than pride and ego.

Forgiveness is the master key in the chain of love that lets us release the pain.

Only after we have forgiven ourselves for our actions and reactions as a child in the psychodrama with our parents and siblings, can true forgiveness towards others take place. We played our own co-creating role with our behavior and conduct, in turn the other family members reacted.

As we become understanding and compassionate towards ourselves, we improve our chances of finally forgiving others. If we remain firm in the belief, that a parent.... teacher....violator.... or in a wider political sense another country....needs to be severely judged, because they - not we - are the perpetrators, then we remain shackled to our restrictions. These "guilty ones" did not have better circumstances than you and I. They had parents, teachers, violators, other countries.... and so on....for how many centuries, even millennia?

Tears of relief stream down your face, when you finally supplant pride with the depth of true forgiveness.

Holding back may be a signal to us that we like living in purgatory. Clinging to familiar aches reveals a tendency towards self-punishment, a self-imposed quarantine from beauty and life-laughter. If you examine the religion you were raised in without blame, you may find the origin for some of these impediments.

Sometimes rituals are helpful in letting go of the old:
➢ Extinguish symbolically the righteous or possessive aspect(s) of a parent or caregiver that hindered your growth. Obtain a symbol for that attitude and destroy it. This ritual will be very helpful in freeing up your withheld love, and for the practical act of forgiveness.
➢ A sentimental item from someone once very dear to you, can be gifted to a nearby river, as an analogy for sending that person now back in their own "river of life", a fond farewell.
➢ You might perform a ritual burial for a former relationship and so on.

Don't be astonished if such a ritual ends in a flood of tears, as you savor the intense love that was smothered by your suffering for so many years.

Our conduct often stems from an unconscious certitude that lessons of suffering have a higher value than learning through love. This mistaken conviction confirms itself constantly in the heartache of daily interaction. This "school of suffering" can be left behind by choosing to learn through love.

One day you discover the "knowing in your heart" about the forgotten truth: all of us have dwelled for lifetimes as a distortion of the love vibration from whence we were brought forth. This "knowing" softens the scars, allowing buried emotions to regain health and become alive in your heart. Now you can start the search for the **materialization of love** at your core, and recreate who you are and want to be.

During this process people experience various pains, possibly needing the assistance of focused body-treatments to loosen physical blockages, which have been stored over long periods of time. Here I have to point out that an almost unbearable pain in the Heart-Chakra can accompany such a profound development. A word of caution: this is usually misdiagnosed by doctors and treated as a stomach disorder.

As patience is the "mother of wisdom", so forgiveness is the "mother of a free mind". So-called stress, hindering the mind's freedom, is mostly our reaction to events around us. Unconscious fear, related to our physical survival, monopolizes our thinking. Another reason for stress is the feeling of "never being good enough", which feeds our old fear of rejection. Some of us may actually fear being "much better" than we let on, which feeds the gnawing suspicion that we are not living up to our full potential.

A free mind, however, cannot prevail without ongoing reflection about actions and reactions as they bestow the values that have been consciously chosen.

Having reached higher consciousness, or enlightenment, the mind remains free, even if momentary circumstances are preposterous. Mindful of one's life-purpose the kind of action or reaction needed is clearly discernable.

A free mind is confident in the here and now. If, upon reflection, a solution can't be found at that moment - at the appropriate time the right situations, words, thoughts and emotions will appear. This confidence of outcome allows such a mind to place occupying thoughts and feelings peacefully aside.

The following illustrates how to begin exercising the free mind prerogative:
> While lying on your back, concentrate on your breath and
> bring your hands together over your lower abdomen as
> shown. Both hands form a female triangle, in the middle
> of which the navel acts as the cosmic center.

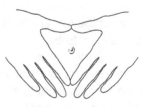

Position of the hands
on the abdomen

In case your inner dialog doesn't want to stop, envision the strokes involved in painting your brain white. You can also imagine a hurricane moving slowly across the weather map of your brain; blowing even stubborn thoughts away.

Meditating in this way enhances inner peace in the here and now.

GETTING CONSCIOUSLY IN TOUCH WITH THE FEELING SELF

Use of the Senses

Training the physical senses, through the tantric disciplines of Yantras, Mantras, Mudras or Nyasas[40], contributes to the mind's freedom while enhancing the ability to focus. These ancient practices have to be adapted consciously in present living if we are to succeed in the tantric way.

Some of these adaptations are already familiar:

Yantras:

- You might have seen a painting, which stirred such deep emotions, that you were pulled into a profound visualization. This allowed your personal symbolism to lead you to a deeper insight of the human essence. While viewing it at length, you plainly surrendered, finally feeling a renewed vitality in your mental and psychological energy.

- You can make your own painting, sculpture or even a patchwork quilt to represent a personal Yantra. Through well-chosen symbols, this work of art shows your own life-philosophy. Personal expression during the creation of such a Yantra is in itself a meditative process. Once completed, this Yantra will always be at hand: gradually intensifying the visualizations you practice to strengthen your willpower. A personal Yantra is a valuable tool when striving for congruence between life-action and life-philosophy.

Mantras:

- You might have sung a snippet of music repeatedly, and noticed a rise of energy in your mood or even in your body.

---

[40]   see page 19

- Consciously forming a short meaningful Mantra for yourself enhances your willpower.

- The Sanskrit Mantra OM (AUM) became renowned in the 60-ties. It has often been consciously used by certain individuals and groups in the Western world to increase the level of energy in the center (3rd Chakra). This Mantra is also used to free the mind, since it enhances the flow of energy from the center Chakra upwards into the brain.[41]

Aura-Mudras:

In our times, almost no one has the patience to sit for hours and concentrate on a classic Mudra. To retain the benefits of the original discipline, and expand it beyond the range of the self, an Aura-Mudra can be created. This remodeled Mudra amplifies the tactile senses and utilizes the energy vibration, naturally oscillating from our palms. The 250 to 300 nerve-endings located on the touching side of the hands are the perfect venue for the coming energy-dance. This rhythmic dance between the hands, and/or extending to other parts of the body, can be used to open the aura especially in those areas where disease has caused a contraction.

The best position for this exercise is the Lotus seat; since comfort is relevant, a full Lotus is not necessary. Start with your wrists resting on your knees, allowing your hands to hang loosely. Calm down by deeply inhaling the prana[42]. Inhale the unseen life-force, and allow it to gather in your lower abdomen. Source your 3rd Chakra, and while exhaling, let the flow of this energy stream like a river into your hands. Focusing your mind for these inner visualizations you are in fact creating nadis. When you achieve even rudimentary concentration, you'll soon feel a perceptible change in your hands: warmth even heat, tingling or prickling, even trembling.

Now start to discern the energy between your hands. Without allowing your hands to meet, raise them and begin to "play" with the energy between your palms. The energy, in the space between the hands, can be felt more intimately through the variable interaction of distance. Alternate the speed of the movements. In forming big and small energy-balls between them, your hands get more and more sensitized. Energy streaming from the fingers of one hand can be received in the palm of the other. Get to

---

[41]   see page 22
[42]   see page 24

know your distinctive energy patterns by checking for differences between the feel of energy beams, as they relate to different fingers. Notice the discrepancy between the energy-flow from each hand as it emanates from the opposite pole.

This Aura-Mudra can be intensified and refined with modifications: Inhale with the focused intention of drawing energy from the earth's center through your Root Chakra into your abdomen, or draw energy from the universe through your Crown Chakra into your center. Proceed with the Mudra as described above. In each variation of this Aura-Mudra you will detect distinctive sensations. Complete this series of exercises by combining them to unify the forces of earthly and cosmic energy.

This is a very pleasant energy-game that also prepares one for a subtle energy-encounter with a lover.

Nyasas:

You can go on to practice the combination of Yantra, Mantra and Mudra, known as "Nyasa". Begin, as you would for the Aura Mudra, in the Lotus seat. This time do so in front of a meaningful painting, or your own creation of a Yantra. After a while start to chant the Mantra OM (AUM), or your own version of a Mantra. As the energy in the abdomen augments, continue chanting without taking your focus away from the Yantra. By use of the nadis, let the energy flow into your hands. Now guide and play with the invisible life-force as you would in the Aura Mudra. Your attention must not divide itself, yet it needs to be applied equally in order to receive full enrichment through the Nyasa.

All these suggestions, as to how you can refine your physical senses, are only proposals. Your creative mind and intuition will come up with your own variations and innovative methods.

Tracing Inner Energy-Motion and E-Motion

To progressively utilize your creative mind, you are required to gradually become independent of others. Internalized "musts", "shoulds" or "have to's" have influenced your actions to an incredible degree. These imperatives pushed and pulled you to act in defined ways and attend established events. In extreme cases new insight may show us that we have never been able to detect our own inner energy-motion. What had to be done, and where it had to be done, was always clear, but how often was it inspired by our own inner motion?

Being free to really do as you please, having full freedom to act - motivated only by your own energy-motion and e-motion - might even confuse you. Doubts frequently come up about "self-sourced" energy-motions or true inner e-motions. "What do I really want?", "What do I really feel?"

Finding out what you want, is easier to accomplish by first sorting out what you don't want. Doing something that you really don't want to do, simply to please others, backfires - even if you are not yet personally aware of this universal principle. As we transition into the Age of Truth, the consequences of this cosmic law become much more apparent in their swiftness and severity. Since my early days as an adult educator in Germany I've reinforced myself with a basic doctrine: Don't do anything that doesn't totally agree with your heart! In the odd case of uncertainty, when I am not sure whether I really want to do something, as the task unfolds, the situation seems to clarify itself of its own accord.

One crucial point needs to be considered during our time consuming search for true e-motions: Psychologically, sometimes to an extreme degree, we are a "product of our family and society", and interact accordingly. At the time of our social conditioning we underwent a subtle learning process. We were taught to use our own brain to manipulate our true inner feelings. With this perverted skill, we became unconsciously proficient in allowing only emotions that were tolerated by those around us to surface. Who could master the assignment of efficiently conforming our internal zeal and emotions to the prevailing values of society better than ourselves?

The true energy-motions and e-motions are at the core. Usually they are smothered by the values, thought-forms and feelings piled on by social conditioning. Digging them out requires clear self-observation, serene self-reflection and above all loving patience.

Internal self-criticism, a by-product of our conditioning, is a troublesome hindrance. Be alert, and remember to silence this criticism, as over the long term it can form an obstacle for personal growth.

Contact with Nature

The sphere of nature does not distinguish between "good" and "bad". The endless cycle of life and death is unaffected by morality. Life is not equated with the positive while death is not linked to the negative. For instance, the lives of flies are important because their death keeps birds alive.

This moral vacuum in nature makes it an excellent space to dwell on life without imposed values, especially the distinction between "good" and "bad" and the resulting value judgments.

Therefore the mind can strive for freedom much more comfortably in nature than it can in an urban setting. In contrast to the city's hectic pulse, everything in nature vibrates without being driven by thought-forms. This encourages profound relaxation.

The natural setting, unfettered by restrictions, is ideal for connecting to your mind's inner freedom and exchanging energy:

Energy-exchange with trees

Letting go of unwanted energy in the form of long standing aches, or suffering can be eased by other life forms, not just humans. In the following naturcise[43], we are going to communicate with trees and ask for their support in this effort.

Find a healthy tree with a strong trunk, gently ask it to receive the painful or as heavy perceived energy you want to release. Be fully attentive to any response: a lack of intuitive resonance would indicate unwillingness on the part of the tree. In this case seek out another tree and ask whether it would cooperate with you in your intent.

When you've found a tree that has shown you a positive inclination - for instance, waving branches or indescribable sensations felt in one of your Chakras - put your back to the tree's trunk. Place the palm of your right hand[44] on the trunk behind you, at the level of your Heart-Chakra.

---

[43] specifically created term, used for exercises of discharging, charging, or exchanging energy in nature

[44] Left-handed persons need to use the hands switched around, according to the principles of polarity.

Put your left palm on your Heart-Chakra. Calm down through conscious breath. As you exhale - bridge the pain from your heart into your left hand. Inhaling, draw the energy through your left arm and across your shoulders. With the next extended exhalation, guide the energy down your right arm and transmit it to the tree using your right palm. Allow this flow to adapt a rhythm: releasing the energy from your heart - guiding it through your arms, shoulders and finally right hand - into the tree. Continue as long as it feels right for you. In the advanced stages of this naturcise, your intuition may perceive suffering from other areas of the body; you can gather these aches in your Heart-Chakra for release. Having brought about your intent, find an appropriate way to thank the tree.

Now look for another tree, one from which you would like to receive energy. Ask this tree to share its energy with you, and as with the first tree, be attentive to the response.

Adopt the same position as above, except this time with your hands switched around. Your sending right hand[45] is placed on your Heart-Chakra, while your receiving left palm is behind you, at the same level, resting on the tree's trunk. While inhaling deeply, take in the tree's energy through your left hand. Harmoniously reverse the direction of the energy flow that was described in the first part of this naturcise. Exhaling, your right hand transmits this energy-flow into your Heart-Chakra, where you absorb it with a long and conscious inhalation. Now breathing out lets you expand this energy into your entire body. Feeling renewed from the tree's energy, thank the tree in your own way.

Energy-Exchange with Mother Earth

Look for a calm place in nature where you can be at ease. Petition this special parcel of earth to foster you in loosening up. Lie down in the "Leonardo-da-Vinci" position[46] with legs and arms outstretched.

Let yourself become aware of the energetic heaviness in your body. Inhale the prana deeply. Exhale generously, surrendering to the gravity of our planet earth. Gift your energy to mother earth and allow her to draw this heaviness out of you. Keep letting go until you feel uplifted and unencumbered. Thank Mother Earth for her help.

---

[45] Left-handed persons: consider the use of opposite hands
[46] see illustration on page 2

Now seek out a new place with a different feel. Here, your quest is another one: ask instead for the earth to replenish your energy. When you feel you've obtained consent, lie down in the "Leonardo-da-Vinci" position, this time on your stomach. Place your head in a comfortable position. The reservoir of Mother Earth's life force is in her center. With an intake of breath, draw a stream of this energy into your Hara - about an inch underneath your navel. When you've felt the spread of this energy through your entire body, you may express your gratitude.

Energy-release on Boulders

Stand barefoot on top of a big rock after being granted permission for the coming energy transaction. Inhale the prana and fill your abdomen with it. During exhalation let the accumulated energy from your Center Chakra flow down. It cleanses your legs of tiredness and heaviness as it passes through the soles of your feet into the rock. Give in to the pull of the rock as it accepts your flood of energy. In sequential experimentation, I have come to realize that rocks and boulders serve as ideal catalysts. On several occasions, major energy blockages were dislodged from my legs and lower abdomen with ease.

Sunrise Energizing

Choose a resplendent site from which you can contemplate the sunrise, stand with your feet well grounded. Prepare through progressively deeper breaths for a very long inhalation. Splay your fingers wide - with your arms and hands straight down your sides. Now breathe in, and slowly with the intake of pure air, raise your outstretched arms towards the sun. Still filling your lungs, your splayed fingers connect energetically with the sun. Drawing your fingers together, you also draw the energy from the sun into your hands while forming fists. The upward angle of your arms, make the energy pour down into your center, while you now hold your breath. With the following strong exhalation, let go of energy blockages, passing them through the soles of your feet into the earth. A boulder underfoot may well serve you as a catalyst.

Instead of the sun you can, for instance, use a powerful mountain ridge as the energy-source.

Sunset Liberation

While watching a wonderful sunset simply stand there, exhaling all your energetic heaviness towards the vanishing sun. Let the disappearing sun take with it some painful old feelings, or use it as a symbol to end a particular phase in your life.

Wave Renewal

Watch the coming and going of waves at the ocean with introspection. You can even become spellbound by the interplay of the currents. Exhale your tumultuous energy along the drag of the out-going waves. Open yourself to inspiration from the incoming waves by gratefully inhaling their enriched energy.

Night-Sky Recharge

Where you can actually see the night-sky, lie down on the earth using the "Leonardo-da-Vinci" position. In a long and profound inhalation, draw on the energy from the universe and guide it into your navel, the body's cosmic center. Exhaling, expand this energy into the rest of your body and allow this universal energy to displace any unwanted emotions. Let this expelled energy be swallowed by the gravity of Mother Earth.

Your creativity will open up many more venues for you to invent new naturcises.

Giving Oneself Inner Peace

Now that you have had intense contact with the natural world, it follows that you've reached another level of inner sensitivity. Being more in touch with yourself makes it normal to seek discovery of your own complete nature.

There is an amazingly descriptive word in German, that a number of Germans have not yet clearly understood themselves:
"Selbstbefriedigung"
"Selbst" = "self"
"befrieden" = "pacify"
"Friede" = "peace"

The roots of the word "befrieden" stem back to the times when one could only feel pacified ("befriedet") behind the protective walls of a castle or town. Refuge was an integral aspect of "Befriedung" - you could not feel at peace unless you were pacified by the safety of the walls. "Befriedigung" is a further extension of this word group and means "satisfaction" in English.

Having looked at the history of the word, we can now discern the full meaning of "Selbstbefriedigung": "giving oneself inner peace and satisfaction in a safe place".

The dictionary definition of "Selbstbefriedigung" is "Masturbation".

I prefer not to use the dictionary when I give myself peace in a protected space. With the evident negative connotations imposed on "masturbation", how can politicians speak of world peace, when so many millions cannot achieve inner peace?

To savor the satisfaction of peace in oneself, tranquility is relevant; so is a space that can enhance the senses.

A Glance at the Female

Tantra views the clitoris of a woman as the northern or forward pole, while the yoni's sacred or G-spot is referred to as the southern pole. The clitoris is the outer part of a flaccid organ, which protrudes from the wall of the yoni. That is why the first inch of the vagina's inner wall is so highly sensitive to the touch. It is the only human organ whose sole function is joy. Swelling to erection through stimulation, this risen shaft can induce an orgasm that opens, furthers, or closes the loop of ecstasy.

The vagina has an area - sometimes sinewy - often bumpy and ridged in texture that differs from the usually smooth tissue. It's size ranges from very small, about the size of a pea, to a variety of shapes and sizes that mostly do not get larger than a walnut. This is the heart of the sacred spot, named in modern texts after the "official" discoverer Grafenberg, hence "G-spot". This spot does not rest on the wall of the vagina, but it can be felt from an area further in, corresponding to the pubic mound. Just like the clitoris, it swells through excitement. Through progressive stimulation, and with improved muscle tone, one finds the G-spot tucked a little further up the yoni. This powerful energy-spot is the ultimate repository for all past sexual fiascos and love wounds. The first profound touch of this sensitive spot is therefore frequently unpleasant and may lead to emotional resistance. It can even be physically painful to find the heart of your sacred spot.

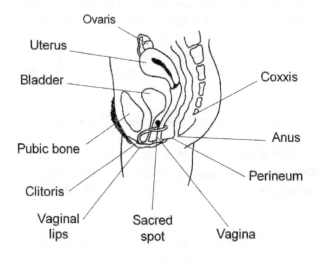

Sideview of female "Sacral Plexus"

Since the sacred spot is positioned close to the bladder, women should fully empty the bladder before touching it; otherwise the excitement provokes the need to urinate. Try to use the ring finger, which is the "sun-finger" or "health-finger", according to Asian palm readings. In ancient Tantra, this finger was prized because of its harmonic affinity with the 2nd Chakra.

Women who have a flexible body can readily stimulate the sacred spot themselves. Many more will have to regain agility in order to reach the G-spot comfortably.

Simultaneous stimulation of the sacred spot and the clitoris escalates the sensitivity. Keep in mind that an over-stimulation of northern and southern poles can cause an energetic short-circuit; forming a new blockage.

Once old wounds have been healed tenderly, the animation of the sacred spot may awaken the dormant Shakti-power - igniting a lantern that throws light on all aspects of life. A woman who has mastered the infinite source of energy, the active Shakti-power, can surrender to the "Wave of Bliss" in a tantric relationship.

An orgasmic woman, consciously aware of her incarnation as a temple of spirit, is wide open to the cosmos. She feels the flow of universal love in her body, being a miniature of the universe herself.

A Glance at the Male

A man naturally has a more relaxed attitude towards his organ of pleasure. The penis and testicles are mostly external, whereas in a woman only the tip of the clitoris protrudes. Urinating several times a day provides routine contact; this does not mean that he is always sensitive to its potential while touching it.

Contemplating the German expression of "Selbstbefriedigung" could lead him to reflect on a crucial question: Do I give my female aspect its rightful place, in this most male of organs, so that I can cultivate inner peace with full intimacy?

Most men have diminished their sexual pleasure through the misconception that an ejaculation is the only signal of orgasm.

Orgasm	for a man is actually an internal experience of the sexual climax.. A vital orgasm builds up yang-energy.
Ejaculation	is merely the external experience of sexual climax: the release of sperm. It usually terminates the orgasm, thus automatically the man yields to his yin (passive) energy.

Tantra differentiates among four successive phases of male sexuality:

1. Sexual arousal
2. Build-up to orgasm/Pre-orgasm
3. Orgasm
4. Ejaculation

When sexually excited, the energy of a man is spread over the entire body, although vortexing in the 7 Chakras. When nearing orgasm, all of a sudden his energy gets concentrated in the 2nd Chakra. This pre-orgasmic phase escalates quickly, and can immediately lead to ejaculation. However, training allows this phase to engender prolongasm.[47] This avoids situations in which a man may ejaculate without actually feeling his orgasm. Tantra particularly emphasizes the 3rd Phase, since experiencing internal orgasm allows men to explore their essence.

A Glance at Both

The premise of a good sexual relationship has to be founded upon knowledge of one's own body. It can only be taken forward by articulating to your lover what you like.

Orgasms can loosen up and dissipate physical energy-blocks. The orgasmic flow can unclog energy channels - and even form new nadis - to a degree of free energy circulation that heals from cancerous tumors.

Energy movement in a microcosm cannot be fully comprehensive, if it has to depend on the stimulation of others. Only by sensing it alone may one delve into the inner energy flow profoundly. Having learned to sense this energy individually, it can now be applied in an "energy conjunction" with another being. Introspective "Selbstbefriedigung" is an indispensable tool for the perception and guidance of the inner energy flow.

Attaining consciousness in every cell, having naturally evolved the body to its purpose as the temple of the spirit, is the ultimate goal of tantric life. In this final stage, one continues to live physically on earth, although without unconsciousness or sub-consciousness.

This domain is not reserved strictly for a few male, and even fewer female Gurus from India. This goal is achievable by everyone who sets out on the path with true willpower. It can change the world.....

---

[47]   see page 103

MAINTAINING AND STRENGTHENING PHYSICAL ENERGY

Intake of Food

A sensitized body becomes more sensitive to the food it receives. For the process of getting sensitized to energy, very deliberate food intake seems unavoidable.

Intake of too much red meat (mostly from beef) hardens the muscles, since the yang/male in food contracts. Furthermore, food grown with potassium-based artificial fertilizers constricts the muscle tissue, while elongating the muscles.

Contracted muscles don't allow the free flow of energy in the body. This makes it more difficult to achieve a highly conscious experience with a lover.

On the other hand, the intake of too many carbohydrates[48] - especially if they are not complemented with complete proteins, including all the essential amino-acids - weakens the muscle tissue. This doesn't enable the body to do "a cosmic dance on earth" any better.

This nutritional conundrum is often evident in those who have chosen vegetarianism. For the first two years, the severity of carbohydrate cravings is not often recognized. It is even believed that solely the consumption of carbohydrates will provide sufficient "energy". After having lived for many years in an industrialized country with a generally too high intake of animal proteins, any attempt at balance is welcomed by the body. Carbohydrates with their strong yin/female character are, at first, a good way to regain yin/yang equilibrium. When however, balance is attained - the body forfeits it through continuous intake of too many carbohydrates. The person

---

[48]   too many = more than 60% of daily food-intake

feels weak, and might often feel pangs of hunger, since carbohydrates are fully digested upon reaching the intestines. The result is frequent cravings for food, and the temptation to indulge is not easily resisted. The body transforms these excess carbohydrates into fat which, as a storage depot for toxins, is often described as cellulite. Another type is beheld on Indian Yogis with flabby fat often drooping over their pants - despite having well trained muscles. The traditional Indian vegetarian diet consists of carbohydrates with a minor intake of proteins. Another sign of this nutritional misconception is apparent in men who form almost female breasts.

Others, convinced that dairy products are the best way to replace meat, increase their intake to a level that prevents health. Dairies are not digested entirely; "leftovers" collect in the intestines, hindering the pumping action of the ring-muscles - further weakening the digestive tract. This restriction denies the body full strength. It also curtails the beautiful expression of physical love.

We have a long way to go before we follow through on the knowledge that dead food, which needs up to 50% of its value for digestion (red meat), is not favorable to the vitality of the human body. To feel physically energized, fresh food-vitamins and minerals are of fundamental importance. Let us also remember the need for sufficient oxygen; delivered by the blood to the various organs involved in the process of digestion.

As you start to proceed on a light-full path, and seek to experience the mystery of life through tantric relationship, you will just get a feeling about the types of food that are not good for you. Your affinity for energy will lead you to the food that can enhance joy in your life. The decision to move at least somewhat away from meat is arrived at more or less automatically.

We still need to learn about the balance of yin and yang[49] in food-intake, which leads to the balancing of contraction and expansion in our muscles, blood vessels and nerves. The physical potential of this equilibrium is found in the art of being tender yet strong in this "temple of the spirit", our body.

Insecure about what to eat at times, you may be drawn to heed a number of available theories being touted about nutrition. Confusion takes place, when so many nuggets of information contra-indicate each other.

---

[49]   see Appendix 1

Listening primarily to the body's inner reaction to food is obviously the best path to follow. The knowledge gained from the observations of your body's reactions allows you to sift through theories with a more relaxed attitude. This is advisable because of the information being continuously collected by scientists about nutritious food intake. The earth's gifts are getting shipped all over the world. We have, at least in industrialized countries, all the material resources necessary to live well even as pure vegans. Deliberating carefully with diversity at our fingertips, we can lighten up our bodies by choosing to ingest only what our particular bodies need; without disregarding nutritional values. Hopefully this will not remain a privilege of the "developed" countries.

In a San Cristóbal hotel room, I once treated an emaciated American woman with a two hour healing massage.

For the first half of the treatment the English word "cheese" seemed to scream out in my mind. The connection to this 52 year-old woman was obvious. Tired of this incessant inner droning, I broke the stillness of the room by inquiring as to whether cheese held any significance for her.

"Chee-eese", the word flowed out of her mouth with a deep warm sigh of relief. "I love it so much, but my diet won't let me have any of it", she added.

"What diet do you follow?" I asked carefully.

"I follow the diet in a book that is supposed to make me spiritual. I really want to live my life more spiritually."

"For how long have you been on this diet?" I asked, respecting her convictions, but trying to find out more.

"For a full year", was her answer.

I examined her body, trying to figure out what might really be going on in her life. It was a skinny gray vestige of a body, appearing sad and love-starved. The bones were sticking out making her figure even more austere.

Cheese, with its very high fat content, would have been plainly beneficial to her - physically as well as psychologically.

Since I was considered as a "spiritually advanced person" in the area, I used the power vested in me to bestow on her full dietary permission regarding cheese. I even suggested that she could consciously confer love to herself, while enjoying her portions of cheese.

She immediately loosened up and was even able to laugh whole-heartedly for the remainder of her session.

Physical Energy-Training

The art and essence of life is best expressed by matching tenderness with strength in your body. Unfortunately, these terms are often confused with "weakness" and "hardness". Exercising the body with only one kind of sport won't keep the body in good enough condition for the journey along the tantric path.

Ancient India focused on a "work-out", which trained all the muscle groups and massaged the inner organs, today we call it Hatha-Yoga. It is a proven method for training the body to be well balanced as a microcosm. Yoga can reinforce the spirit's temple and make it a refined base from which to experience the cosmos.

Hatha-Yoga is taught throughout the Western world, however one need not master Hatha-Yoga to accomplish effective body-training for a tantric way of life.

Nonetheless, effectively rendered asanas[50] combine conscious breathing with physical exertion and internal energy guidance, which is essential.

Kundalini-Yoga, a much later development, trains its focus on the raising of Kundalini-energy. Tai-Chi emphasizes the inner energy-flow, with much less regard for muscle training. Complementing it with Hatha-Yoga is an excellent way to fuse the disciplines for maximum benefits. Shii Soei Ching training - integrated with the physical practice of Yi Gin Ching (parts of the complex art of Qigong, also called Chi Kung) may be an ideal configuration for the tantric way of life. This meticulous discipline, however, needs profound devotion. Certain martial arts can be adapted to reap the benefit of building muscle tone while consciously breathing and guiding energy through the body.

Specific Muscle Training (Pc-Muscle)

Vigorous muscle tone is a sought after commodity in Western traditions of sport and physical fitness. One very neglected muscle does not fit into any recognized training schedule. The fitness of this very same muscle

---

[50]   positions of Hatha-Yoga

allows us to exercise the ability to vault the dimensional gap between humans and the universe.

The name of the Pubococcygeal Muscle gives us its position: stretching from the coccyx to the pubic bone. Cradling the sexual organs, urethra, rectum and anus, the Pc-Muscle is actually an entire muscle-group, joining the sacral plexus (1st and 2nd Chakra). This Love-Muscle has a key role during sexual enjoyment and ecstasy.

There has always been a simple technique for gaining awareness of this muscle: momentarily cutting off the stream during urination. Whether you knew it or not, the clenching compelled the Pc-muscle to tighten around the urethra.

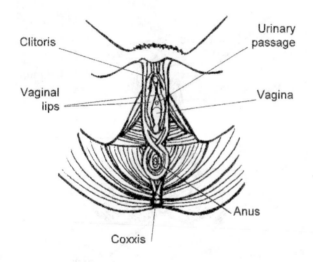

Female Pc-Muscle

To strengthen this muscle, practice interrupting the flow a few times, each time you urinate. Having gotten a feel for the Love-Muscle, you can revitalize it by alternating rapid contractions with a full relaxation of the muscle. You can do this to the rhythm of music, while sitting in a subway or at your desk. By pressing your heels into the ground while sitting, you can intensify this exercise. Contract the muscle while inhaling (women may also imagine drawing their yoni up towards the heart during contraction). Holding the breath and the contraction progressively is highly effective[51].

---

[51]   This also helps to lift a heavily collapsed uterus. Combined with other

During exhalation total relaxation is necessary, to avoid a stiffening of the Pc-Muscle. Rigid Love-Muscles not only induce tension but also retain it. A Pc-Muscle that matches tenderness with strength provides one with the necessary suppleness and agility for ecstasy.

For men, the inner clenching also provokes outer movements. Practicing these subtle motions alone can be enhanced with imagination, for instance, to picture the pleasant slide between the inner vaginal lips and the clitoris. With further exercising of this muscle, the contraction can press the penis forward. Imagine using this pumping response for refined penetration. The slight movement becomes more palpable with continued conscious breathing.

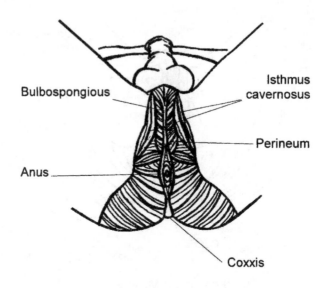

Bulbospongious

Isthmus cavernosus

Perineum

Anus

Coxxis

Male Pc-Muscle

When male or female Pc-Muscles are well defined, it is possible to feel the delineation from the other muscles in the area.

The Pc-Muscle is a major muscle group, responsible for the contraction of all ring-muscles in the yoni of a woman. A dynamic Pc-Muscle can induce a powerful orgasm, increasing the potential for multiple and extended

---

"Kegel-exercises", an operation can be avoided.

orgasms. With a vitalized Love-Muscle her yoni's individual ring-muscles can be brought to bear separately.

Women can test the strength of their Pc-Muscle by inserting their index and middle fingers in the yoni. A vigorous Pc-Muscle can easily press open fingers back together.

Giving birth is usually much easier with a well trained Pc-Muscle. By exhaling strongly with an attitude of "letting go", orgasms can be felt as the Love-Muscle encourages the child in its natural progression from the womb.

An active Love -Muscle in a man enables
➢ strong and firm erections,
➢ the re-channeling of accumulated sexual energy in the 2nd Chakra back into the other Chakras and the entire body, thereby
➢ prolonging the orgasm,
➢ facilitating the separation of orgasm from ejaculation.

A vital Love-Muscle in either sex
➢ stimulates blood circulation and
➢ may help maintain the immune system by increasing the flow of white blood cells[52].

A weak Love-Muscle can
➢ cause lower back pain,
➢ lessen resistance to certain diseases in the genital area[53]
➢ hinder access to the sacred spot,
➢ often contribute to chronic tension and/or depression.

Avoidable influences that weaken the Love-Muscle:
➢ remaining in a sitting position for extended periods
➢ the intake of sugar, white flours or excessive carbohydrates, especially if accompanied by a low intake of complete proteins
➢ intake of too much food with yin character[54].

---

[52] White blood cells fight infections. People with AIDS often have low white cell counts, and reactivating the Pc-Muscle is especially important for them.
[53] i.e. yeast infections, vaginitis, collapsed uterus for the female, hormonal problems or cancer of the genitals for female or male
[54] see Appendix 1

DIRECTING MENTAL ENERGY

Different forms of meditation are practiced by quite a number of people at present as they seek inner peace in the Western world. It frequently helps them to relax and free the mind, and often to find solutions to mundane problems.

Meditations can raise your energy level. Over time, they may help you get in touch with your inner energy-motion and e-motion. Meditation is a tool for shedding light on your spirit's purpose and path on earth. Many people have experienced during deep meditation sudden insights into one or more former lifetimes. The *samsara*[55], and the karma connected with it, can be discovered through a series of meditations. By knowing and understanding one's *samsara*, a person can transform karma into dharma. Doing this while on earth is the way to free oneself from the obliged cycle of material existence.

Meditation has been used in India since pre-history. When the physical movements of Hatha-Yoga are correctly practiced with simultaneous meditation - it is "body-meditation".

In general, meditations are begun with conscious breathing. To a yogi, the meditative control of the breath, combined with the conscious use of the Chakras, is the mastery of life. Yogic breathing relaxes the physical body, the subtle energy body and the mind. It influences the energy-flow between all three of them.

Here are a few meditations, which may help you to find and maintain the unity of spirit and body.

Wave-Breathing Meditation

Lie down on your back with legs slightly apart, the arms relaxed at the sides of the body though not touching it. Start with deep and unhurried breathing to calm down.

---

[55]   the entire cycle of reincarnations

Inhale the prana - filling your abdomen with this breath of life... let the wave of energy rise to your chest... and lastly fill your shoulders with this undulation.

With exhalation - empty the tide of energy from your abdomen... then feel the wave leave your chest... and finally release it from your shoulders.

In this dynamic meditation, one does not interrupt the flow by holding the breath. Repeating the cycle of breath while gradually intensifying it, builds the wave motion from your abdomen through to your upper body.

Feel the coming and going of the wave, which brings in new life force and cleanses out the old.

Sunrise-Meditation

Lie down in the "Leonardo-da-Vinci" position[56]. Now move your arms downwards, half way back to the body, let them rest there. Slow down your breath while deepening it.

Imagine yourself standing somewhere in nature, watching a beautiful sunrise. Take a deep sigh. Then draw the light and warmth of the sun into your Third Eye with a lengthy inhalation; let it flow down until your abdomen is filled with the warm light of the sun.

While exhaling pour this light forth, filling your body until you can beam the energy from your foot-soles, toes, and fingertips, and finally from your head using the 7th Chakra as a focal point and the hair as tiny emitters.

Use this meditative process to imbibe the sun's light in your body. You will be more aware and conscious of your body, as your body becomes more enlightened.

Should you, at a later stage, want to advance the enlightenment of your body, or even heal a sick organ with this meditation, extend it as follows:

With a long and strong inhalation absorb the light of the imagined sun through your Third Eye and let the river of light flow down into your body's

---

[56]   see page 2

center. There, it is enriched with your own substance and empowered by your will[57]. Exhaling, expand this energy from your center to your entire body. Repeat this procedure a few times.

Then guide the energy with your focused mind through different body parts. During all these sequences, recharge your abdomen by drawing on the light of your visualized sun with inhalation, before sending energy forth to another place in your body.

Exhale the light energy from your center down your legs, funnel it through your ankles and rebound it outwards through the bottom of your feet and toes. Pay attention to the energy-flow with your mind, and loosen up energy-blocks in your legs by consciously beaming the light-full energy through their dark density.

During further long exhalations, guide the light-full energy into particular areas of your torso: the genitals, intestines, kidneys and bladder, stomach, liver with the gallbladder, pancreas, spleen, heart and lungs. When you send the warm light of the sun as healing energy into your heart or sick organ, concentrate especially on releasing the pain through exhalation. Let the powerful beam of light stream through the dark knots of energy until, with a few more concentrated breaths, your heart and/or sick organ can shine with light.

Exhaling anew, conduct the light-full energy up your spine through your neck and light up your head with it. Let your eyes shine with the light. Channel the light through the debris in your ear canals, and sensitize your ears to the truth. Blow the energy through your nostrils. Send it from inside your head into your mouth, enlightening it. When guiding this energy into the lips, bestow them with alertness to the food they take in.

Having cleared the senses, during your next inhalation bring the enriched energy from your abdomen up into your brain, and displace old unwanted thoughts, spiraling them out through your 7th Chakra.

Finish with an integration. Inhale, funneling the warm light of the visualized sun through your Third Eye. At first, let your abdomen brim

---

[57]   In the navel are the direct descendants of the very first cell of your body, wherein you brought – at the time you were conceived - the enormous willpower required to live this life.

over with the energy, as it melds with your substance. Now, with a long exhalation, expand this light energy to fill your entire body. Enjoy this cycle a few times until you can feel the beams of energy seeping through your foot-soles, toes and fingers, and emanating from your 7th Chakra and hair.

This involved body-meditation can lead to high consciousness in the body.

Meditation Unifying Body with Spirit

Our body is energy, materialized from the earth's substance, while our spirit is energy linked to the universe. The soul/psyche is the transmitter, providing our bodies with movement by linking us to the universe. This is background for the following practice of meditation.

Lie down on your back in the "Leonardo-da-Vinci" position, with your arms stretched out at an angle that feels comfortable to you.

While inhaling, you draw energy from the center of the earth up into your Hara[58] on the back side of your body. During exhalation, expand this energy out to your entire body.

Then, with the next inhalation, you draw energy from the universe into the cosmic center of your body (navel), again expanding it during exhalation.

Now combine the action by inhaling the energy from the center of the earth and the universe into your Center-Chakra simultaneously. During exhalation, allow the fused energy of the earth and the universe to broaden across your whole body.

This meditation harmonizes the interweaving of body and spirit, and usually helps to strengthen willpower. You may discover many more positive aspects resulting from this meditation.

---

[58] the body's earth-center, about one inch below your navel

Chakra-Meditation

Lie down on your back with legs slightly apart and arms by your side. Relax and get into your body with gradually deeper breaths. During inhalation draw energy from the earth and universe into your Center-Chakra through Hara and navel as described in the previous meditation. When exhaling send this energy down to your 1st Chakra, the coccyx.

Focus your mind, and give over your senses to your 1st Chakra:
a) take the time to feel it thoroughly,
b) visualize the Chakra's color and/or range of colors, as you become conscious of the shapes they come in, allow them to form freely and intertwine with each other in movement,
c) focus your inner ear to your Chakra's sound, perceive the tone or melody,
d) smell the scent of your Chakra, perceive the flavor of it.

Once these sensual phases of the 1st Chakra have been experienced - with the following long inhalation raise your focus and send your energy to the 2nd Chakra, realizing the exploration there.

Follow this process, traveling through all the Chakras until you have gained sensual, visual, audible, olfactory and taste awareness of each one.

Now with a long and profound exhalation, journey from your 7th Chakra down the spine to the coccyx. Inhaling deeply, direct the flow of energy - with this new sensual awareness - through all the frontal Chakras up to the 7th Chakra. Exhaling, let the energy stream down your spine into the 1st Chakra again. Allow this complete cycle to flow as long as it feels right to you. At a certain moment you may, however, feel that you want to reverse the direction of the energy flow; Inhaling, your energy flows upward in the spine and exhaling, it passes downwards through the frontal Chakras from the 7th Chakra to the 1st Chakra.[59]

During this final part of the meditation, keep the inner cycle of energy going through the Chakras, thereby freeing them and stimulating their energy.

---

[59] One way practicing this energy flow is Buddhist practice, the other way is Taoist practice.

When first sinking into this meditation, you will remark that the completion of it takes training. To start with, you may focus on only one, or a few Chakras, until you feel comfortable with concluding the entire meditation. Allow yourself to see the change in the chakral colors. Since life is constant movement, at times our feelings vary, causing variations in the chakral and aural colors. This same principal is valid for the other senses. Observe your own process, as you gradually progress through these partial meditations.

You have the option of placing your palms up, open to the input of the universe, or seeking a connection to the earth by laying them downwards. It would not be surprising, if you perceived - to some degree - a difference in the sensations of your Chakras, according to the conscious position of your palms.

"Inner Flute"

The Chakra-Meditation can be folded into the "Inner Flute", a tantric meditation that is often performed in the Lotus position[60].

Focus your concentration on one of the two Chakras, which form the sacral plexus: the Earth-Chakra at the coccyx - or the life-creating Sexual Chakra at the genitals.

During deep breathing, cycle the energy through the individual Chakras as described in the final part of the Chakra-Meditation. Once the flow has been established, you may use this energy-flow to "touch" a chosen Chakra, according to the focus of your mind. Like playing a flute you can choose to "open" or "close" the note or energy swirl of one or more Chakras. Exhaling opens a Chakra, sending forth energy. Inhaling closes a Chakra, keeping, or drawing energy in. You can "finger" all 7 Chakra notes and choose to combine certain Chakras through breathing.

It is advisable to be very conscious of which Chakras you want to leave open and which ones you want closed after this meditation. Take into account the sensitivity of open Chakras, when you finish your "playing of the flute".

---

[60]   see also drawing on page 84

Finally, raise through a long inhalation the energy from the sacral plexus up to your Crown Chakra. A focus on sexual energy during this meditation may, at this point, spark a bolt of lightening in your brain. This mind-blowing experience might lead you to view the world in a different way.

"Cosmic Intercourse"

While our Crown Chakra is energetically linked to the universe, our Base-Chakra is connected to the earth's center. This arrangement makes our bodies a three dimensional pillar between the two elements. Through meditative breathing, and utilizing the position of the spine as an axis linking earth and universe, Yogis and Tantrics have long practiced "Cosmic Intercourse" in their physical and subtle bodies. The time-honored position for this countercurrent of energy is the Lotus seat.
-      Inhaling, energy is drawn down from the universe into the 7th Chakra.
-      Holding the breath, energy is guided down in the spine to the coccyx.
-      Exhaling, energy is transferred down into the earth.

This classical "Cosmic Intercourse" may also be reversed to raise earth energy up into the universe.

The energy can also be sent both ways during the course of the same meditation with a break in between. First, energy is drawn down and given with thoughtfulness to the earth. After a while, energy is drawn up from the earth while inhaling and given mindfully to the universe during exhalation.

The original "Cosmic Intercourse" can also be used to simply draw on universal or earth energy, and expand it in the body.

It can also be used to inhale universal energy into a part of the body which needs healing.

ᑕᓄᗷᓄᑕᓄᗷᓄ ~

Once you have enriched your existence on earth, you will get a significant clue to the meaning of the expression "all the universe swings on love-vibrations". Firmly on your path, learning about your own energy, and life-energy in general, you might honestly feel, that all you **are** is love. This leads you to wonder about the tangible deformations of love all through the social world. Deep anxiety - the dominant emotion in the Age of Darkness - has pretty well left you, as you increasingly became your Self. The depth of confidence, manifesting itself in your daily life, was heretofore unknown to you. You will notice that you can disentangle yourself more easily from the worldwide web of destructive vibrations.

Choosing love as the basis from which to learn your lessons, you will now harvest rewards in your daily life. "Human understanding" and "compassion"- not to be confused with false harmony, achieved by taking on a psychodrama-role for the sake of other persons - are then not merely words used to impress. Even your bodily movements will be a physical expression of love, truth, humility and compassion.

It will no longer make sense, neither physical nor verbal, to hail someone's attention, simply to satisfy momentary needs and desires.

You will **be**,
simply your Self.
As this truth of you,
your Self
is uniquely attractive.
You will not need to do anything about it.

As an entirely logical result, the right partner or partners cross your path, and in their company you can share the journey of discovery, with its lessons and purpose on earth.

THE TANTRIC RELATIONSHIP

PSYCHOLOGY OF A TANTRIC RELATIONSHIP

Biological Basis for Sexual Dichotomy

The most sensitive body part of a woman is internal, thus naturally the feelings connected with it are very intimate. A man's equivalent body part is mostly external, and thus he does not as readily internalize his most intense sensations. Men also have a very sensitive spot inside their body: the prostate gland, reached from inside the anus. Many people have no knowledge, and even less awareness of this sensitive male area.

Women, who have yet to discover the sleeping beauty of their vagina, think that their clitoris is their organ of ultimate sensitivity. Although the sole function of this organ is pleasure, clitoral orgasm alone does not allow a woman to open herself as wide as the universe. The much more complex sensitivity of the yoni needs to be involved before one comes to such uplifting milestones through sexual union.

Because of the internal aspect of the yoni, the woman's sense of intimacy with her lover is of great importance. If she doesn't feel intimate with him, she can't overcome hindering limitations, and open up to him and his entering of her. If she does not sense his intimacy, she can easily feel abused. Since, during intercourse the woman has to open her body to allow a part of a foreign body into her, she has a factor of self-protection built into her natural psychological "pattern". Originally, women were also designed with natural caring and concern for a healthy genetic connection, in case of possible pregnancy. Over thousands of years, having been overpowered by patriarchal behavior, she has lost touch with her own nature.

A man, whose obvious sexual organs are "extensions" of his body, even handled during simple urination, does not naturally tie many feelings of intimacy to it. Therefore tantric practice teaches a man to consciously connect the Sexual Chakra with the Heart-Chakra, enabling him to communicate intimately with her. If he cannot achieve a satisfying relationship with her - inasmuch as she can't open up without feeling his intimacy - his lingam easily becomes nothing more than a "shooting gun". Because of her nature, he is then often rejected by her, frequently in a very general way. This "frustrates him to death": giving him the psychological push to work out his problems as a violent man who kills. This process is not restricted to individual cases, as world history and our present time illustrates.

Psychodrama and Former Lifetimes

Each partner in a relationship brings to it their own social programming. In their interactions, once in a while some old wounds can get opened, even if both have already done a lot of "letting go" and conscious "new programming".

Be careful in such situations lest your ego becomes involved and you start to blame; stimulating the guilt-circle that frequently spawns an endless spiral of destruction.

Trying to subdue your ego you could be tempted to avoid conflicts. This however, can actually be worse, keeping one in the spiral of destruction. Conflicts, at first perceived as uncomfortable, give us - in the search for equitable solutions - the chance to grow permanently out of pain, ergo through conflict we can achieve true harmony.

We have had in the Age of Darkness excellent training by reliving endless cycles of guilt. Now it is up to us to interrupt, even in the most banal situations of daily life, this vicious circle of destruction. Understanding, that almost no one alive today has not killed someone of the same species in a former life-time, one can bring to new light religious concepts like "original sin". The time has arrived to free ourselves from the negative spiral, irrespective of its source, and live our true nature, materializing our capacities as cosmic beings on earth in a life-creating and beautiful form, sharing, caring and loving.

The "Field of Love-Expression"

Partners create their "field of love-expression" together. The dance of love can take place in a beautiful garden, or it can float like free energy in the universe. In any case, we all would prefer a dance of love to a battle of the sexes.

Battlefields are associated with death. Fields of war in a love-relationship break open old wounds - the resulting emotional withdrawal can inadvertently lead to the rejection of all love vibrations. Without a rekindling of the spark of love, emotional death may ensue.

In contrast to false harmony through the avoidance of conflict, true harmony and confidence towards the partner is the psychological basis - essential for the mutual creation of a beautiful field of love-expression.

The level of psychological and energetic freedom that each partner brings into the field of love-expression is of special importance. Hence, let us observe the different stages that the two partners may come from.

Let's consider the woman:

Her psychological and energetic stage of freedom is in tandem with her level of Shakti expression. Shakti is the most intense life-energy. Its scope of embodiment is coarsely differentiated into five levels of "body-fires" in women.

non- or pre-orgasmic:

Never having had an orgasm, often the woman is unsure, whether she even knows what an orgasm feels like. Her psychological background, allied with social programming, has formed a network of energy-blocks on the physical level that prevents orgasm. In the West, the abundance of superficial sexual information has made many women in this stage skillful in pretending orgasm; they know that he needs her orgasm to reach closure.

Most women never have the chance to grow beyond this level of Shakti expression. You may wonder how widespread this stage is still today. Twenty-three African countries still practice female genital mutilation, countless other women live in sexually oppressive societies. Projections of a probability-rate as high as 90% worldwide may not be exaggerated.

seldom orgasmic:

These women are in a more receptive position, and sometimes able to let go. The natural "high peak-time", coinciding with their 10 hours of fertility in the menstrual cycle[61], and the pre-menstrual period, are the two phases during which it is easier for them to open up. I know indeed some women in different countries who have only been one time sexually with a man – and they are mothers.

orgasmic:

Having found out which types of kisses, positions and movements are most enjoyed and can "trigger" their orgasms, these women have gotten an idea of how potent the energy of Shakti can be. They are also content to interrupt a love encounter, mainly when they see that their partner is tired or feels less energetic than themselves (in most cases when the man had had an ejaculation).

poly-orgasmic:

The lives of these women already transcend the normal, and during their serial orgasms the intensity can climb to ecstasy. Bountiful passion, expressed at a level of uncommon intensity can eventually lead to the "State of Bliss" in the extended orgasm.

amrita orgasmic:

This extended orgasm allows women to adventure into an openness to, and of, the universe. In an amrita orgasm women reach up to seven peaks of ecstasy, each one generating a higher crescendo. Mounting the final pinnacle of ecstasy, she releases amrita, which may be considered as "female ejaculation".[62]

A woman capable of extended orgasm can also release amrita in situations other than sexual ones. For instance, when having orgasmic feelings while sitting in a tree or lying on the earth. Whenever she feels open like the cosmos, she easily surrenders, thereby ushering in the release of amrita. This sense of unity with the universe, felt in her entire

---

[61]   see Appendix 2

[62]   Tantric life was so commonplace for the spiritual elite in ancient India, that even towns were named in reference to tantric practice: i.e. "Amritsar" in the North-West of India, or "Omkareshwar" (= "fiery lingam") - a pilgrim's town located between Agra and Bombay.

body, can be triggered anywhere on her skin - simply by a soft caress from fingertips filled with consciousness.

Amrita is excreted from the Bartholin's glands, also called the "female prostate glands". These small glands are on both sides of the lower part of the vagina. Amrita is a milky, or light and clear, liquid that evaporates quickly. To expel it from the Bartholin's glands, the urethra is brought into play. According to tantric texts it is highly nutritious, both physically and psychologically.

Liberating as much as a full cup at a time, a woman may "ejaculate" several times during a single love-meditation. The tremendous life force behind this beckons the analogy of an erupting volcano. Amrita springs forth like a geyser reaching crests as high as six to seven feet (2 meters).

A Brahmin in Varanasi performed a worship ceremony on my body; calling forth both "Kali" and the "White Goddess", in order to combine and unify East and West. Suddenly a cool liquid was poured between my legs. Convinced the Brahmin had poured the sacred water of the Ganges on me, I was somewhat concerned after the worship about any ill effects of the dirty river water on my genitals, even though it had obviously disappeared. When I queried him about it, his eyes took on a strange look as they met mine, since the water of "Mother Ganga" is holy to devoted Hindus. Slowly the Brahmin revealed to me, that it had not been Ganges water but my own "amrita", which had squirted so high, that by the time gravity had splashed it between my legs it was no longer warm. Only then did I recall that during my state of trance I had felt an explosive breakthrough in my lower abdomen.

Let's consider the man:

A man is much more than a functional organism, ruled by a brain that can sometimes be subjugated by a "sperm-shooting" penis - a perception that so many women are tempted to believe and may unconsciously fear. Both, women and men, just need to learn on a discovery-journey, how intense, full and beautiful men can be as a microcosm, a whole Self that uses brain and body according to his authentic desires. Then the man's part in co-creating the field of love-expression will be welcomed by a woman.

Men who have done enough work on themselves are more in tune with the universe; this no longer allows for the build up, or continued existence, of an unhealthy ego, steadily needing to be confirmed, even - or especially - in bed.

At the developed stage, a man realizes the unity of everything existing and his role in it. When this knowledge is buried in the unconscious, a man might try to fulfill the longing for a lived awareness of this union by ending up in bed with lots of women, dispersing his energy and going nowhere. A wise man knows that everything intertwines, living one great unity as a part of the One - propelled by energy that has no beginning and no end.

This wisdom can be distilled from the field of love-expression, where a man may experience the wide openness of the cosmos through a woman's ecstasy.

Ejaculatory control[63] allows a man to feel his internal orgasm, thereby enjoying the powerful energy-current flowing through his body. He may even feel a strong vibration take over his entire body, and have the chance to transmit this energy to the woman, exciting her and satisfying her soul. A lack of ejaculatory control bores and frustrates an orgasmic woman and in extreme cases, may even make her angry.

No longer ruled by his lingam, he consciously chooses the best use for his orgasmic energy. By realizing this freedom of choice his over-all life improves, he is empowered. A man normally looks and feels younger, when he has more orgasms and less ejaculations.

The decision to lengthen an orgasm - by withholding an ejaculation - should not be taken, when the semen is underway. Interrupting an ejaculation can cause bladder infection, and may also lead to a constraint of the prostate gland, which over the long term may even develop into cancer.

Women can help men to ejaculate with control. Her extended ecstasy can contribute to his higher self-esteem, so that he doesn't even feel that much need for an ejaculation ... ...just to want to stay in an orgasmic state. This creates an opportunity to drop his ego, discovering simultaneously his female side. In nature, the male ego is a necessary device for the survival of the species. Today however, this very ego stimulates violence and armed conflict. Ejaculatory control and the resultant strengthening of the female aspect in men could finally lead us away from the plentitude of guns and wars in the world.

---

[63]   see page 103

PRACTICAL PREPARATIONS FOR A SEXUAL LOVE-ENCOUNTER

Time and Space

To live ecstasy and magic in a sexual union, life in general needs to be organized in a way that allows space for conscious loving.

Conscious loving cannot be accomplished by "rushing it through". When the mind is harried by commitments because "this" or "that" still needs to be done, the field of love expression remains barren. It is not advisable to squeeze in 20 or 30 minutes, in order to follow the instructions of an exercise in conscious loving.

Life moves at a much faster pace than it did during the zenith of ancient Tantra. Today, everyone is involved in a multitude of social interactions. If you want to cultivate real growth in your field of love-expression, you may have to schedule your time for ecstatic love-encounters.

A room full of chaos, or at the opposite extreme in rigid order and cleanliness, does not supply the basic comfort level a tantric relationship needs. Somehow we all know, that the surroundings we create for ourselves are a mirror of our internal state. The more your love-expression has opened you to the universe, the more your space will change.

A tantric relationship can flourish best in a room free of outer energy-input, since in our time energy is so often used destructively. A room, equipped with everything you wish to have there to enhance your feelings of conscious loving, is significant. Being as unique as we are, and differing so widely in our feelings and tastes, rooms suited for conscious love-expression vary:
- To one couple it's important to have a room with wide and open space like the cosmos, adorned with only a comfortable mattress and carefully chosen music.
- To another couple the coziness of a tiny room augments the sense of safety.

- Some partners initiate the ritual of conscious loving in a room that contains not only drums, flutes and other instruments, but also feathers and other accessories that will enhance their excitement and ecstasy during the love-dance.
- Other lovers prefer to be somewhere in the great outdoors, reveling in the green of nature while inspired by the background of flora and fauna, and being soothed by the sound of water.
- The beach, or the top of a roof beckoned by the night-sky, are further examples of countless possibilities.

In case the couple lives together in a continuing relationship, a special room decorated according to their own sense of beauty serves well for profound love-expression. When both partners have grown into microcosms, each of them will have their own space, from which they can invite or visit each other.

Mental, Energetic and Physical Cleansing

A conscious love encounter thrives - contrary to spontaneous sex - in a space that has been prepared for delight. The body and mind also need to be brought to readiness, to enable an opening up for an encounter with the whole Self of the lover.

For many of us, "bed-acrobatics" just don't do it any more, for others it has never done it. We want to find completion as an authentic Self, and from that center intimately express our feelings. Quite a number of people wonder how this could be possible, when being forced to spend so much energy by participating in society just to sustain one's material existence.

Of course, the best and most healthy way to receive everything we need to maintain our physical existence is by serving the world with those skills we enjoy the most. This concept is what the Sanskrit term *arth*[64] means. In employing this talent for others, we are best be served by it.

Although, if we live ideally by our talent, stress and strain through the interactions within our present world are hard to escape.

---

[64]   see page 30

In the Age of Darkness there is often a habit of using alcohol or other drugs, to enhance the illusion of releasing the stress of work. This relaxant effectively lowers inhibitions and is frequently used as a "stimulant" for a sexual encounter. Meanwhile we can learn to consciously choose what we imbibe.[65]

If you want to free your mind from the strain of a hectic day, start by closing the door of your workplace behind you. Stop for a moment after closing the door and give yourself the time for a conscious departure. Don't carry the problems with you, since the solutions won't be found, if your mind is continuously caught in the problems. Then put this "leaving behind" into physical action, taking each step consciously as you distance yourself from all those problems. When you notice that you are breathing afresh, start taking your steps into fuller life in view of your whole Self - not your work-activity, which is only a part of you. If you have the option, choose the most beautiful route to go home or to the place, where your love-encounter will be.

You may, at this point, feel badly in need of a bath or shower. We have learned to think that a bath only entails a cleaning of the physical body, however many of us have already experienced other beneficial effects. Clean water helps us carry out a psycho-hygienic as well as energetic cleansing. This bath may help you remove the mask you had put on for the people at work and kept on during your commute. In washing everything off, including unwanted thoughts and feelings, you become free to find more ritualized ways to purify yourself. Naturally, everything is immeasurably more effective, if we do it with consciousness.

Perhaps you noticed on your way home from work, that your body automatically started to breathe more profoundly. Take this opportunity to deepen your breath and draw the life-energy into your physical body. Start to stay with your breath and use it to enhance the awareness of the present. As a further step, focus on your breathing, and utilize it for psycho-hygienic cleansing.

Feeling pure awakens the desire to be beautiful and to experience a splendor of senses with your partner.

---

[65] Actually, frequent drinking of alcoholic beverages often causes impotence.

Pure truth is beautiful, real beauty is inexorably linked to truth. The distortion of truth deforms beauty. Emotionally in the midst of this malformation, many of us struggle when hearing, seeing and feeling the truth. One frequently prefers old habits and patterns rather than overcoming fear towards the unknown. We go through a phase of sadness, when we realize how long we have hindered real beauty in ourselves and in life - by not delving into the unknown and coming face to face with the truth.

Your intuition will connect you with the enhancements the world offers to your senses, now that you are in tune with them and their interplay. One truth of nature is that the original odor of our bodies is pleasing to the senses. It's just that almost none of us, in this deodorized society, has ever detected this fact. Intake of unhealthy food creates a discrepancy of balance, which cannot be smothered by fragrances. The programmed insecurity concerning our physical bodies has spiraled us down, until we can no longer perceive the beauty of our own nature and our natural intuition.

My first days in the New World were spent in the Grand Canyon, an area I later described to a German friend as "the place of the perfect materialization of love". From there my path led me to the tribe of Rolling Thunder in Carlin, Nevada.

To my surprise, the tribal rules were quite rigid and repressive - far from exemplifying the Native American philosophy I had read about, and been so attracted to.

I was apparently a threat to the tribal leaders, because I refused to toe the line with my thoughts and feelings. Looking into people's eyes - specifically if they are of the other sex - was forbidden according to the tribal regulations, another rule I would not follow. Therefore, I was refused permission to go for a walk with the only other visitor to the tribe, a male journalist from Florida. Not intending to break any more rules of the tribe, I went for a walk on my own. He must have done the same thing: arriving from opposing directions we met, by so-called coincidence, at a nearby creek. Laughing at the irony, we began to share the shock each had experienced during these last few days visiting the tribe.

Sitting there, exhausted by the heat and releasing the accumulated emotional tension, I just let myself fall backwards to the dessert floor. A wonderful scent surrounded my head. The journalist, detecting a fragrance from where he was laying, followed the scent to my head, giving me a kiss.

We burst into a deep and full laughter, since the tribe had done everything in its power to avoid this "sin"...

Synergy between the Lovers

The Tantrics of ancient India usually ritualized the preparation and form of sexual union. Although the event itself was an act of meditative concentration, once underway, the union of spirit and body was fully spontaneous in its expression and movement. The couple moved out of space and time, feeling eternity as they tuned in to the vibrations of the universe.

To reach out into these areas of experience, it is necessary to vibrate on the same wavelength as your partner. This was not as much of a problem in ancient times. In a single cultural background, life did not "swing" on as many wavelengths, than it does in today's multicultural societies, which meld so many different races of varying energy-input and wave-lengths.

It's important for a couple to consciously "synergize" their vibrational wavelengths.

If one of the partners is running at a high, while the other partner is on a low frequency, they may not find ecstasy together until they synergize. There are people, who are always on a high frequency, while others are consistently in a low frequency. It's not advisable for these opposite extremes to form a couple, unless both of them are ready to welcome the unavoidable alteration of frequency - should the energetic correlation succeed. Beware, since a sudden drastic change of frequency has the tendency to bring on disease.

ENTERING THE LOVE-DANCE

There are thousands of ways to enter the encounter, which exemplifies our most profound feeling for life: love.

The Nurturing Dynamic[66]

If one of the two lovers feels drained by something that has happened during the day, the Nurturing Position is a wonderful way to synergize. For this position both partners lie down on the side in spoon fashion, the stressed one on the inner, nurtured side. Of course, the dynamic should be comfortable for both.

The Nurturing Dynamic helps
➤ to create the harmonic balance necessary for adjusting separate wave-lengths in order to eventually vibrate at the same frequency (synergize)
➤ to stimulate the energy-flow in the bodies of the partners
➤ to align the Chakras.

At first it is best to **breathe rhythmically** together. Inhale, hold the breath, exhale and pause together repeatedly. Then the partner, lying behind the other, transmits energy from his/ her own Chakras into the backside of the nourished partner - while exhaling with emphasis. Ideally, the flow of energy transmission is guided to the equivalent Chakras of the recipient.

After a while, the back of the inner partner - who had built up tension during the day - gets softened. The recipient of this freely given energy can let go of tension and psychological pain more effectively by exhaling through an open mouth, even sighing at times.

---

[66] I need to admit feeling a certain resistance towards the word "position" in the context of conscious loving. Love-expression is so full of inner and outer movement, that the static term "position" appears too restrictive to allow a good description of it, so I have decided to replace it with "dynamic".

Spoon-Fashion

To fortify the process of letting go, the partners can proceed into another version by use of **reciprocal charging breath**. One lover exhales while the other one inhales; both partners pausing simultaneously - one with full lungs, one with empty lungs. While inhaling, the nurturing lover charges him/herself with energy from a chosen resource: *Prana*, the image of the rising sun, a spring, energy from the center of the earth or energy of the universe - there are no limits for the creative mind of a loving person. Being so close physically, the receiving lover inhales the enhanced energy of the exhaling partner. Even after feeling that this dynamic has been completed, it is not advisable to switch positions. The originally stressed partner is still in the process of letting heaviness go outward through exhalations. This process sometimes continues on very subtle levels, and the now restored lover would not want to take the chance of having their partner be the recipient of any discarded energy.

It is very important for the giver to draw on energy from an outer resource, in order not to deplete the personal energy level. A limitless resource also allows for a much more powerful energy-transmission to the momentarily weakened lover. Having received this energy-boost, the body of the person who had felt worn out starts to regain vitality - the positive feelings for life spring forth, and the mind is set free to enter another dimension.

Both partners have been influenced by this caring energy flow, feeling a calmness that has the anticipation of excitement. The free flow of energy creates a feeling of lightness and leads to the aura's expansion, individually as well as couple-wise.

Couples can also ameliorate health by loosening energy-blocks with reciprocal breathing. It's possible to deal with past trauma in this Nurturing Dynamic, working through the old pains, feeling them consciously again until - without forcing the issue - you remember that

> you are now
> the one
> who chooses
> how to act, react and interact
> and
> how to guide your own life
> with
> regard to outside circumstances
> appreciating their lessons
> while
> becoming conscious that you are
> your own creator.

The Butterfly Dynamic

My introduction to this dynamic came during the first healing treatment I performed on this continent – it was fully clothed and non-sexual. I make this point only because it is important to remember that Tantra is a life path in which sex is an integral tool, but not an end in itself.

This dynamic is a good way to let go of suffering and at the same time feel nurtured by a loving partner. As one lover lies down, he or she places the head so that the 7th Chakra points to - and connects with – the sacral plexus[67] of the other one. The Butterfly-Dynamic encourages a deep calming effect in the whole body of the person being cradled.

During exhalation, the horizontal partner may guide energy through his/her Crown Chakra into the Sacral Plexus of the sitting lover - who simultaneously inhales, drawing it up the spine and out through the own 7th

---

[67]   1st and 2nd Chakra, see page 10

Chakra, when exhaling. The Inner Flute channel is especially well suited for the flow of energy, which this reciprocal breathing sets into motion.

Butterfly-Dynamic

If the partners are well versed in the practice of Inner Flute meditation, the experiences in this position can be fathomless.

If the woman is the sitting partner, the negative pole of her 2nd Chakra allows her partner to free himself from serious back-pain, which is merely the result of blocked energy. In this reclining position, his back relaxes and the energy blocks start to soften. Inhaling powerfully, she draws the energy from these loosened blocks up into her yoni. Guiding it through her Inner Flute, or using the nadi of her spine, she frees herself from this energy through her Crown Chakra during exhalation.

Feeling the Inner Flute

To the sitting lover deep satisfaction arises from being able to give their partner sensitive warmth and protection. The vertical position does not overpower the stretched out lover, but rather empowers the sitting partner, who may experience their full existence and enjoy the freedom from taboos.

At some junction, the vertical partner may have the inclination to lie back while going through such intense concentration. This fully horizontal variation of the Butterfly-Dynamic can allow them to fuse their "Inner Flutes", leading the lovers into a special cosmic experience.

Heart-to-Heart Salutation

This greeting is an age-old ritual, which prepares the soul for an encounter of love.

Clothed or naked, the partners sit facing each other in the open or closed Lotus-seat, and bring their palms together in front of their Heart Chakras, in the manner of the classical "Namaste" salutation used in South East Asia.

Heart-to-Heart Salutation

Slowly revealing their eyes to each other, taking the time to gaze deeply into the mirror of the partner's soul they recognize each other profoundly without words. Appreciating each other's distinctiveness by respecting the equality of spirit, they behold the depths of their loved one's heart. Yielding to the attraction, they can gradually allow their foreheads to meet, and rest together calmly. Secrets of the heart may be shared in the act of connecting to each other's "true seat" of human intelligence[68].

My last year in Germany was spent in a beautiful, joyous relationship with Johannes. With my full agreement he used this relationship to overcome some burdens from his past - even though he knew from the first day on, that one year later I would be somewhere in the Americas.

Late one afternoon, he suddenly asked me to do him the favor of going over and sitting on the mattress …he wanted to see something. Automatically taking the Lotus-seat, I sat down there and he soon joined me. We faced each other in the faint light of dusk. Anticipation about what

---

[68]   Ancient Egyptian texts refer to the heart as the true seat of human intelligence.

would happen kept my eyes fixed to his face. Without even blinking, I let a sigh escape, which brought on another state of consciousness.

In that instant, countless faces rushed across mine - altering my countenance with incredible speed - faces of women, young and old, from times and cultures that spanned history. It was an extraordinarily subtle sensation, when just some of my many facial muscles fluctuated just a tiny bit here and there, as each face, and a knowing about the life it belonged to, came and went.

Johannes in the meantime was greeted by a display of faces from Egypt, India, Turkey, Africa, Russia, Greece, the pre-Columbian Americas and numerous other cultures. Acknowledged by these women young and old alike, his own face went through a rush of awareness, eventually taking on a strange blend of expressions, ranging from doubt to openness to incredulity and astonishment. His perplexed face shimmered through the veil of female history that was gliding over me - until the muscles on either side of my mouth pulled a smile onto my face. I could no longer hold back the imminent burst of laughter that brought me - the woman present in this life and time - back to reality.

The abrupt ending of this "multicultural review of history" caused a fit of anger in Johannes, who, understandably, just did not want to let it vanish from his sight.

Exchanging Energy through the Hands

Opening up to each other can be very subtle if the lovers begin their dance from a distance, delving into it slowly, with an energy-exchange through loving hands.

The partners sit facing each other according to their preference (dressed or naked) in the Lotus-seat, their hands loosely dangling from the knees. At first the eyes work better closed, inasmuch as the focus is directed inward. Both partners concentrate on breathing slowly and deeply. Exhaling they guide energy from the Center Chakra into the hands, sensitizing them. Getting a tactile sense of the energy, they start to play with the energy-field between their own hands. Familiarized with the vibrational sensations, they can intertwine their energies in a four handed quartet.

Allow this initial energy-connection with your partner to lead wherever it is heading. People often skip over subtle energetic encounters in their haste to reach defined goals. Don't risk cutting short the beauty of a discriminating love-vibration by rushing intercourse. Letting yourselves get there by following the energy flow - rather than forging ahead - leads to much higher experiences later on, but faster than you think.

You can initiate and intensify the energy-flow between the hands, if you inhale while using one or more available sources:
- draw energy from the center of the earth in through your Base-Chakra and up into your 3rd Chakra,
- receive universal energy through your Crown Chakra, guide it through your spine down into the Center-Chakra (principle of Cosmic Intercourse)[69],
- absorb the warming light of an imagined sun into your Third Eye, let this energy flow down into your abdomen,
- fill your center with life-laughter

Aligning the Chakras

A further possibility, for evolving the "deep and high" encounter, entails the partners sitting in the Lotus-seat while beginning to concentrate on their own Center Chakras.

Breathing reciprocally, each lover sends energy from the 3rd Chakra to the partner's 3rd Chakra - who receives it while inhaling. The lovers may combine the energy swirl of the Center-Chakra with that of the Heart-Chakra, thereby bringing their whole Solar Plexus into play. Exchanging their fountains of energy so intimately allows them to start surfing together on the same energy-wave. At a later stage, you can also add your Sexual Chakra to the fountain - opening the gateway to erotic encounter.

The Yab-Yum Dynamic

The Yab-Yum mode is widely practiced, however the potential enhancement of a relationship through its wide range of energy dynamics is still a mystery to most. *Yab-Yum* means unification of father and mother; the original significance denotes him as the creator while she gives that creation its actual form.

---

[69]   see page 66

This dynamic can also be used in the first strides of the love-dance.

The woman sits cradled by the man's thighs, both lovers having first come to an agreement on the type of breath and internal concentration they will practice. This is one of the most intense co-meditations: both focus on their Inner Flute, moving the energy consciously from the Root Chakra to the Crown Chakra. Together they can now form an energetic pillar. They also can enhance and transmit the energy of each Chakra through reciprocal breathing.

Yab-Yum Dynamic

Suddenly, totally different "pictures" and perceptions of yourself and your partner can come up. You might see your own and/or your partner's former lifetimes. A flash of light may fill your vision with your partner's aura, or you may experience yourselves as a big expanding light. These are only some of the avenues of learning available to couples, if neither holds back by staying in heavy feelings of the past or by constraining the future with expectations about the outcome of this meeting of the souls.

I had just started my sojourn in San Cristobal de las Casas in Southern Mexico, finding accommodation in a wooden hut on the only hill "Rancho San Nicolas" had to offer. One morning, I was awakened by enchanting flute music echoing throughout the valley; a very pleasant introduction to the day. Repeatedly, the high notes sent me into the sky like a bird, soaring above of the forest, and the low tones glided me to a soft landing on a bed of warm earth. Lying there, I never wanted this flight of bliss to end. Finally giving in to curiosity, I stood up to search for the source of this beautiful music. From the vantage-point of the window, I could see a young man, standing like a pillar in front of the only hut next to the ranch's entrance. The sound of his flute wafted upwards. It seemed, that his entire existence and high spirits were being portrayed in this poignant music, which touched me to the core of my existence.

On my way to town an hour later, I had to go by his cabana just to leave the ranch. From his vantage-point, now sitting on the bench, he could obviously see my entire body's smile, and smiled his own welcome to me. He introduced himself with his spiritual name, "Siddharta", but mentioned later that he was baptized as "Alberto".

It did not take too many days for us to move beyond idle chatter, and one candle-lit evening found us in the Yab-Yum Dynamic, swinging our bodies together in a harmonic rhythm.

Holding each other close, and even breathing in unison, we instinctively let ourselves fall backwards with a long sigh. Our cosmic centers connected with the energy of the universe, shifting my sense of vision to a place, where I could perceive multiple dimensions.

Sitting up again in slow motion, the face I encountered sprang forth from long forgotten history books. It was undoubtedly that of Ludwig II, a Bavarian king who was never understood by his contemporaries, although today one of the four extravagantly built castles, he left to posterity, is famed throughout the world.

Being born in Bavaria, I'd already had several experiences with the energy, surrounding this castle Neuschwanstein, as well as at the lake in which Ludwig II had met his end in 1886. Oddly enough, even German tourists notice the similarity between the lay of the land in San Cristobal and southern Bavaria.

Tenderly communicating my recent vision to Siddharta, I surprised him with the news that he was probably the reincarnation of this Bavarian king he had never even heard of.

Dance

Dance has always been an expression of spirit, and it remains a joyful way to approach your love for the encounter. You may try pausing during a passionate dance, and initiate a sensual dance of the sacral plexus'. Bring your hips into a swinging motion and liberate your 1st and 2nd Chakras by swaying the sacral plexus to and fro, and undulate in rhythm with the sacral plexus of your partner.

Having become familiar with the Inner Flute, you can allow the stimulated energy to rise in this channel upwards to the 7th Chakra. Continuing this dance, you can create a swirling pillar of vitality that energetically connects earth with universe. Use your intuition to bring into play your aura and make this gambol colorful and uplifting.

Like all the suggestions in this book, these are only ideas. Your own creativity will find many ways to express your love, once you've opened the gateway.

TANTRIC TRADITIONS OF SEXUAL LOVE-EXPRESSION

In tantric love-expression the physical senses are fully used for the enchantment. Since ancient times, traditions of kissing and conscious touch have been passed on. These were enhanced by sounds, eye contact and visualizations and further combined with conscious breathing, which was of special importance.

Being fluent in body energy, having the capacity to prolong orgasm, knowing the magic of certain movements and positions seemed unavoidable for the attainment of ecstasy in the mystical cosmic experience.

Traditions of Oral Stimulation

The most common form of oral love-expression is a kiss on the lips. This simple touching of lips can open a myriad of possibilities: tender lip-touch, kissing above and under the lips, licking the lips, tongue and upper palate. The kiss of some is like a sip from the "spring of life".

Little "love-bites" can be taken in a soft (yin) nibble or in a strong (yang) manner. Light sucking and elusive blowing are genteel caresses.

Kisses lose their charm when done technically, with the mind or the eyes elsewhere, since the receiver can't help noticing their superficial character. Delving into the feeling, without concern about whatever might present itself, is the attitude that initiates pleasure. Kisses with this approach can stir up the energy in the body and release energy from the Crown Chakra to the body. Sensual kissing of the Chakras, enhances the energy vortex and may ease their opening to energy resources.

A conscious kiss under the upper lip can be felt all the way down to the genitals, as the energy flows through the major nadis stimulating the 2nd Chakra. Gently nibbling on her inner upper lip, using his tongue and lips to pull slightly on the frenulum, triggers this internal sensation. Most of the time, she will respond by playing and sucking with his lips. She may visualize her energy as it streams from her stimulated gums down via the nadis to her clitoris; this may readily bring about a clitoral orgasm.

The stimulation of the upper palate - which the frenulum and upper lip connect to - inspires the release of a warm liquid, which originates in the 7th Chakra[70]. Suddenly lubricating the mouth, it is often mistaken for saliva. According to ancient tantric texts, this volatile fine liquid comes from the subtle body. They consider this as the **1st peak of "Libation"** i.e. releasing energetic liquid, which nourishes the receiver and stimulates the vitality of the giver.

Kissing the forehead at the Third Eye can help it to open up for a clear view through the illusion around us, and the situation we have put our life into. This might eventually lead to the capacity of seeing into other time periods and former or future lifetimes.

Kissing and lipping the ear area can cause a rush of energy through the entire body. More precisely, this can open up rarely used energy-channels, running from the ears down to the Center Chakra. From this cosmic center of the body, energy can "shoot up" so intensely across both ears (sometimes intersecting at the Heart Chakra), that it then bursts forth, leading into intensely across both ears (sometimes intersecting at the Heart Chakra),

Center Chakra funnel, using ear-nadis
and Thousand Fold Lotus

---

[70]   apparently from the pineal gland

Center Chakra funnel, intersecting at Heart Chakra
and Thousand Fold Lotus

that it then bursts forth, leading into an opening to the universe. The energy from the universe, usually felt at the 7th Chakra, now takes over your whole body, involving the two ears and using the cosmic center in the 3rd Chakra as a funnel point. This experience has brought me to a better understanding of the ancient tantric symbol of the Thousand Fold Lotus on the 7th Chakra.

Thousand Fold Lotus
on the 7th Chakra

Leaving the house of two elderly Jewish women living in Mexico, I felt the first headache come on since having left Germany years earlier. It had been a nice respite, but now my head was close to exploding, and I only made it home by forcing myself through the cloud of pain while trying to ignore the hammering in my head.

A few minutes later an unusually tall Guatemalan I knew, who had moved here from Antigua, rang my doorbell. He had come to schedule an appointment since phones were a rare commodity in San Cristóbal. Realizing my predicament, he soon left - giving me a sensitive kiss on my left ear to say "good-bye for now". This tender transfer sparked a bolt of energy that shot from my ear - right down to my Center Chakra, where it augmented my strength in an instant. From there, energy shot up just as quickly, but now into my right ear. When he had left, this energy-triangle - formed by my 3ʳᵈ Chakra and each ear - opened up to the universe and gave me a feeling of absolute endlessness.

The word "Shiva" entered and refused to leave my mind, I felt a strong resonance to the word although I had only a suspicion of its future significance in my life.

Two days later, bending over to brush my hair, I glimpsed my head in the mirror through the A-frame of my open legs. The shape of my hair falling down that way astonished me, as did the word "Selket" which immediately sprang to mind, even though I had no idea of what it meant.

Within the week, one of the Jewish women finally succeeded in her attempts at lending me a book about Tutankhamon. While perusing it at home I actually came across "Selket". It turned out she was the Scorpio-Goddess of ancient Egypt. Being a Scorpio myself, I was not surprised about this recent weaving of the energy web. Discovering the nuances of all these cosmic bandhas is a life-long ambition of mine.

The **2ⁿᵈ peak** in the release of the **"Libation"** or **"Nectar"** can be climbed by kissing the woman's breast's and nipples. A direct heart-connection between the partners can be made in this highly erotic encounter. It is not common knowledge that breasts - in such an intimate heart-connection - may secrete libation. This subtle fluid can be slightly milky or salty-sweet, although in toxified bodies it may have a dark-greenish tint.

Kissing the breasts of the partner, regardless of sex, can be intense therapy. People, who were not or not properly breast-fed and/or manifested eating disorders in the first year of life, are prone to addictions like smoking, alcoholism, and adult eating disorders. The resulting unconscious pursuit of emotional nourishment is very common in the psycho-dramatic framework of adults in industrial societies. Admitting to yourself that underlying emotions are so closely bound to the first months of life, you can then enter into the full enjoyment of kissing and being nurtured by the breasts of the lover.

The nipples of men are very sensitive, yet some men have never discovered this. They may be uncertain of how to react to the tender kissing of their nipples, and even less certain of the enjoyment it can engender. As a man, you can consciously nurture your partner, and in giving her the solace you've longed for, you can start to heal some of those deep wounds in her and yourself.

The healing effect of kisses can be extraordinary. A Mexican lover of mine had, from a severe eating-problem in early childhood, a physical manifestation that prevented him from controlling the muscles around his mouth. Even though he had lost feeling in his lips, one night his intuition led him to passionately kiss my sore neck. The endless lipping sucked out the energy blocks from my neck, which had been heavily injured in a car-accident 15 years earlier. Although excessive stress still causes minor discomfort, my neck has never been a source of agony since that night, which also brought healing to him, when his mouth regained feeling and muscle control.

All these "oral traditions" were considered sacred rites in Tantra. These rites can be transformed into healing rituals. Tender kisses may unblock tight thighs and free the hamstring muscle from painful tension, and may even heal the sexual Chakra in women and men. When kissing the Sexual Chakra we have to remember that our programming caused for many of us a widespread denial of the 1st and 2nd Chakras. Therefore, at first it is advisable to maintain a lot of visual contact with your lover during oral sex.

When fondling or suckling the jewel (clitoris), be careful not to block the energy flow through over-stimulation. This always short-circuits the energy-fluidity of a woman. Wanting to please their partners, lots of men tend to do this when aroused.

She can kneel over her outstretched partner, offering him her jewel and yoni as she seeks out his lingam with her mouth. If she no longer holds men responsible for her orgasms, she can take this opportunity to start a pelvic dance, increasing the excitement with her lover. Having reversed the position, he offers his genitals to her.

Through the oral stimulation of the 2nd Chakra the **3rd peak of "Libation"** can be attained. For thousands of years this "nectar" has been considered as a special "healing balm", for the giver as well as the receiver. It is potent and can be swallowed as a medicine. This clear liquid has no similarity to men's ejaculation or women's amrita.

Another "oral tradition" of Tantra entails the drawing of energy from the Crown Chakra. During orgasm she lifts her tongue gently to the roof of her mouth. This releases a "fountain of energy" from her Crown Chakra down to her tongue, more intensely if she keeps her tongue on her palate during the entire length of the orgasm. Then, she can offer him her tongue to suck on. Over this connection, powerful energy is transmitted to him. Using inner visualization, he can channel this energy down to his lingam; that way his penis receives this intense energetic charge. Having accumulated the energy there, he can transmit it back to her from his 2nd Chakra into her yoni. Through contraction of her Pc-Muscle she can pull this energy up in her body, this is much more effective, if she inhales profoundly. Of course, some practice in the conscious use of mind-power is helpful.

Conscious Touch

Conscious touch leads to an awakening of energy and to the possibility of directing its flow. The more consciousness is put into the touching hands or fingertips, the more effective they will be for energy stimulation and guidance. Energy does beam out of the palms and fingertips, and even if only the aura gets touched, the flow can be felt by a sensitive partner.

According to Tantra,

Touch can be

> stationary or dynamic
> gently pinching, squeezing, scratching
> brushing with the fingertips
> carefully tapping or slapping

Touch is of

> different speed and has
> different levels of firmness

Touch

> with a hand whose energy flow is intense can
> lead to the experience of an "unknown realm".

If your partner seems nervous, lay your hand on him or her, and slowly start into a caress - an excellent way to calm your lover down. If your partner is very calm, almost boring, begin with a slow tender touch, matching it to that person's momentary vibration; deepen it gradually into a higher speed. For a touch to be welcomed and considered as "good" by your partner, you need a certain understanding. Communicating your compassion while caressing your lover, you will somehow identify with them on an inner level and be able to reach that understanding. Don't confuse this with losing yourself in the psychodrama of your partner.

The large variation in the degree of touch can illustrate, how fine the line is between pleasure and pain. In the Kama Sutra one finds descriptions of yang touch and "love-bites", actually drawing blood. These can be used for the sake of freeing energy that has been solidly obstructed. One might begin to look here for an understanding of the aggressiveness[71], that is sexually expressed in sado-masochistic relationship.

Placing our hands, as opposite poles, on any of the seven Chakras, we can use the energetic flow between them to open up sluggish nadis in our lover. Besides having an emotional effect, the influence can be intensified if both lovers breathe reciprocally. Most important is the exhalation, which supports the releasing of energy. For example, the woman can lay her left hand on her lover's genitals, while her right hand is lying on his Heart Chakra; exhaling she sends energy of love out of her right hand and into his heart. Inhaling, and using her negatively poled hand, she draws the accumulated energy from her lover's Heart Chakra down to his 2nd Chakra.

Touching gives you pleasure, even more so when the partner receiving it is open to your caress. The lover's openness is a gift to you, and the joy is enhanced as the giving becomes more and more mutual.

A touch with the intention to take, easily leads to a "harvest" of internal rejection; this is usually not perceived as long as the one-sided energy transfer lasts. Therefore be careful, lest you repeat the old hurtful patterns of your childhood and/or former relationships. In such a situation, the blossoming of unnecessary roughness, either physical or verbal, is a simple barometer.

---

[71] "Aggression" comes from the Latin "agredere"; the neutral definition is: "to go towards the world", a necessary virtue for survival.

Approaches to Conscious Touch

Touching the Woman

➤ "Jewel in the Crown"

Either partner maintains finger-contact to the clitoris with a gentle pressure. The consciousness in that fingertip determines the profoundness of the sensation. If she has awakened her Shakti, there is no necessity to move the finger(s), because her own pelvic undulations will arouse the jewel.

➤ Simultaneous Touch of Clitoris and Nipples

Tenderly touching the clitoris and playing with the nipples at the same time, gets many women "warmly" aroused. Experimenting with the poles can open new nadis.

➤ Touch of the Sacred Spot

A liberated sacred spot lets the woman respond openly, unlimited creativity in the touch can then be explored. Since an unencumbered G-spot has the effect of allowing a free flow in all the energy-channels of the body, the possibilities in cosmic love-encounter become endless.

➤ Joining the Northern and Southern Poles

His index and/or middle finger act on her sacred spot, while his thumb arouses her clitoris. The flux of energy between her poles can electrify her pleasure.

Touching the Man

➤ "Playing the Flute"

Finger the penis with all the awareness in your finger-tips, and play his lingam as you would a flute.

➤ "Ringing the Lingam"

Let your fingertip(s) and thumb meet in a ring, which embraces the penis, and follow the shaft up and down. From the most gentle (yin) to the most firm (yang) movement, you can alternate by putting the emphasis of touch into different fingers, since each of them has a significance of energy, which is connected to a planet.[72]

➢ "Holding the Wand"

The fortification of a partially erect lingam, can be done energetically by embracing it gently with your positively poled hand. Sending energy across the palm of the hand to the penis, especially when it is directed underneath the frenulum, can easily stimulate, although the hand isn't even moving.

➢ "Namaste" Position

The woman honors the erected wand of light, enclosing it with the palms of both hands. Concentrating, she can close her energy-circle between her hands, and send the energy of her microcosm across the penis. Another meditation can occur if she uses her breath to draw on energy from a source. Having accumulated energy, she can exhale and guide it from her Center Chakra through her arms - beaming the energy to her lover from honoring hands.

Simultaneously touching:

Tapping or rubbing the lingam against the genitals, or even around the anus, of the woman can be handled by either partner. A slow speed can build, as contact between the first two Chakras varies from gentle to firm to gentle again.

Whenever you feel like it, let your hands assist you in giving pleasure to the Sexual Chakra and sacral plexus.

Usually, touching herself to induce orgasm in the act of love, highly arouses her partner. Excited by the feeling and observing, he also blossoms in the explicit understanding, that each lover is taking responsibility for their own orgasm. Sadly, women still fall into the trap of avoiding this; assuming it may affect his self-esteem.

72

Thumb	= Venus	= life-intensity, erotic, logic and willpower
Index finger	= Jupiter	= "I am my own creator"
Middle finger	= Saturn	= influence from outside: both social world and universe
Ring finger	= Sun	= light and healing
Small finger	= Mercury	= wisdom

Outer peace is dependent on inner peace. As a matter of fact, a lover-relationship is much more satisfying when both partners know how to give themselves inner peace[73].

Importance of Eye-Contact and Visualizations

In Tantra the eyes are considered as a mirror of the soul or as a gateway to the soul. They are the main source for an opening towards intimacy.

Through the eyes, we readily transmit energy from our Heart Chakra to another person. Eyes also receive energy from the Heart Chakra of the partner. Naturally, eye contact is the beginning of the love-encounter.

The sending and receiving functions of the hands can be trans-located to the eyes, since they also are poled. Of course it follows, that left-handed persons have to send and receive in diametrically opposed directions. Intensified through an exhalation, energy of the heart can be beamed to your lover through your sending right eye. Focus on the left receiving eye of your inhaling partner.

These suggestions follow the classical pattern of giving, sending and the external guiding of energy, while exhaling
correlating to
drawing, receiving and the internal guiding of energy, while inhaling.

Consciously unfurling his Base Chakra, while drawing energy from the center of the earth through it and up into his eyes, the man projects this energy into the eyes of the woman during his next exhalation. Her accepting inhalation of the energy "grounds" her. Note that the poles of the eyes have been omitted, since it is also possible to send or receive with both eyes at the same time.

Converging her attention, even to the point of sensing her heartbeat in her Sexual Chakra, the woman can draw this sensuality up into her eyes. From there, she now beams this energy into her lover's eyes while she is exhaling. Drawing in his breath, he welcomes the passionate radiance of her gaze.

---

[73]   see page 48

A glance filled with the deep intent of your Center Chakra, where earth and universe converge, can empower your partner. A strong exhalation by the giving lover, while the receiving one draws this energy in, intensifies this gift of energy.

Visualizing a powerful source of energy, allows you to gather the endowments of this energy - and lovingly send them to your partner during eye contact. She or he may actually get a glimpse of the source.

Sound Enhancement

Once you've fairly dissolved the energy clot in your Throat Chakra, sounds may just slip out of your mouth. Sound off to your partner, make your preferences audibly clear. From moan to screech, the vocal range is as limitless as the variety of yin or yang degree in kisses, touch and movements. You can even intonate the speed of movement.

Don't make artificial sounds, or the sounds you assume your lover wants to hear. The insincere resonance will only superficially arouse your partner. You deceive yourself, as well as your partner, ultimately reaping pain that often remains concealed in unconscious perceptions.

Let the sounds, which reverberate from your depths, surface externally through moaning, whimpering, growling, crying, screaming, howling and laughter, even singing. This stimulating "concert to the love-dance" has a profound intimate meaning.

Words could suddenly be too harsh. The magic spell of primal sounds gushing from the depths of your real emotions may vanish in the mists, if you narrow your experience by saying, "I love you". You will sense that your whole Self is expressing your love through your body and energy - "speaking" the truth much better then words ever could.

Words mechanically uttered out of habit or aloofness just for the partner's sake, will, rather than please the partner, cause more hurt feelings and an internal withdrawal. Despite this, in cresting the summit of fervor, words may just spring forth - and your lover will know the truth by the vibration of these verbal tidings.

"Speak for pleasure, speak with measure,
Speak with grammar's richest treasure
Not too much, and with reflection-
Deeds will follow word's direction".[74]

Quite frequently, men seem to have more difficulty in letting go of sounds. Although sometimes women may feel frightened when a "beast-like" sound breaks out of a man in a volcanic ejaculation, this fear is overcome by the understanding that energy-knots have just been spewed forth.

Welcome all sounds, which are truthfully given. Some may be a "universal cry".

During a two-week sojourn at the home of a Japanese woman friend in Tepoztlán, (1½ hours South of Mexico-City) a group of her friends came to visit one evening. A man with a huge fresh scar on his face was among them. Four weeks earlier, this Colombian had been run over by a speeding ambulance, and left for dead on a deserted Mexican highway.

As his story unfolded, the eight of us got into a heated discussion, and it took some time before we drifted apart into three smaller, more intimate groups. The sound of multicultural dialogues spread like the harmonious humming of a beehive. The energy was palpable - it seemed to vibrate throughout the room - as we all sat around on various pillows and blankets.

The Colombian and I had paired off to form one of these groups, ending up in a conversation that was getting more and more intense. An electrifying tingling was felt in my Solar Plexus, as the energy-flow between our Center and Heart Chakras grew torrential. Energy-currents swung back and forth between our bodies, finally reaching an unknown, indescribable peak of density. With nothing left for words, they faded away.

Twelve years later, I still remember the dense "cloud" of energy that enveloped us, as we meandered into another room. Our physical unification sent my mind into the infinite - my senses followed - diving into the abyss and climbing the peaks of ecstasy. All of a sudden, a subterranean rumble began deep in my abdomen, and with a powerful upward movement it burst through my throat dispersing with a blast of ultra-deep sound. In the

---

[74]   Panchatantra, page 247

moment of its leaving my mouth, I reached full awareness of it... realizing that this sound had come from the depth of the universe itself.

To this day, the internal shivering and shaking that was the aftermath of this episode continues to be felt on occasion.

Conscious Breathing

The relief that sound can bring, has a lot to do with the energy release of the breath that expels the sound. A constricted Throat Chakra does not allow sounds - connected with true feelings - to make it through without getting distorted. If you become conscious of restrictions in your 5th Chakra, exhaling with enough focus can liberate the passage.

When you are halfway into orgasmic peak, inhale very slowly, then extend your exhalation with lots of sounds. The volume of sound and depth of the orgasm are mutually influenced. This leads to longer orgasms and little by little even to better lung capacity. More lung capacity leads once again to a fuller, richer volume of sound.

In loosening the 5th Chakra this way, the energy-flow is usually guided "south" into the body's 2nd Chakra. With a further deep exhalation, this "river" can be encouraged to head "north" again, even into the 6th and 7th Chakra.

Focused breathing during sexual encounter can be done yourself, or in tandem with your lover.

Alone or in unison, the vibration of accumulated love-energy can be sent - using a long, goal oriented exhalation - to a sick person or even countries at war. If the ecstasy of two lovers is sent out that way, it is called "Red Tantra".

Prolonging Male Orgasm

Focused breathing is of major importance, if a man wants to live ecstasy. Opening himself to the full realm of orgasmic possibility means learning and practicing the art of "prolongasm".

An observant and sensitive man has noticed four phases in his sexual encounters:

1st Phase: Sexual arousal
2nd Phase: Build-up to orgasm/Pre-orgasm
3rd Phase: Orgasm
4th Phase: Ejaculation

When a man feels his body going into the second phase, everything speeds up fast. In the first phase all the Chakras are affected, "turned on". In a moment, all the energy is funneled to the 2nd Chakra. Simultaneously, the other six Chakras and the body are energetically discharged, while the Sexual Chakra nears flash-point, the so-called point of no-return.

At this point, Tantra teaches to redirect the current. In this way the energy is brought consciously back into the body and its Chakras while inhaling strongly. Practice is necessary, if one desires to completely master his ejaculations. According to ancient tantrics, in this mastery lies the power of self-transcendence.

The methods of reversing the river of energy from the 2nd Chakra into the body and the other Chakras are internal (based on breathing, training of involved muscles and focus of mind) and external (practiced through conscious touch).

Internal Practices to Prolong the Orgasm

➢ Control of the Breath
Slow, deep breathing:
Yogis are trained to hold back the ejaculation by use of breath control. Nearing ejaculation, the speed of respiration naturally increases. A conscious slowing and deepening of the breath in such moments slows down the second phase of the sexual response pattern. Breathing in tandem with the partner intensifies the effect.

Desynchronize Breathing and Motion:
Breathing normally during coital movements lets the man exhale when pushing forward, and inhale when moving backwards. Close to the point of "no- return", exhaling while pushing forward leads fast to an ejaculation. Therefore tantrics either exhale in the opposite way or completely desynchronize their breathing from their movement.

Inhalations by Steps:
The man draws some air in while pushing forward, then the breath is held while pulling the lingam back. After repeating this for a few times, a long exhalation follows.

➤ Relaxation of the Cremaster
At the point of "no-return" the scrotum shrinks through the contraction of the cremaster which brings the testicles close to both sides of the base of the lingam, forming a strong erection. That way the penis is set ready to ejaculate. Tantrics relax the cremaster (= muscle in the scrotum) to stay in the orgasmic state.

➤ Focused Shift of Energy to Higher Chakras
The energy is guided by use of mind-power, nadis and breathing
> from the 2nd Chakra
> into the Heart Chakra,
> then into the 3rd Eye,
> then into the Crown Chakra

This energy shift can be brought full circle, leading the energy from the
> Crown Chakra in the spine
> into the Base Chakra,
> then into the Center Chakra,
> then into the Heart and Throat Chakra.

➤ Guiding Energy into Hands and Chakras:
With a focus-shift, and a long intense inhalation, the man guides the energy from his 2nd Chakra either up into his Heart Chakra (expanding it that way that the energy flows to his hands) or to another Chakra of his choice. Eventually with inner serenity, he feels the energy-vibration, and so does his lover, as he transmits it to her. The variations of giving modes are many-fold, and increase when the couple interchanges the energy through different hand and Chakra combinations.

➤ A fourth internal technique for redirecting the accumulated energy from the Sexual Chakra is practiced by bringing to bear the pubococcygeal muscle, whose training was described above (see page 56).

External Practices to Prolong the Orgasm

➢ **The Press of the Perineum**
A slight press is applied to the man's perineum in the area that covers the internal penis. This unseen lingam is imbedded under the testicles and continues back almost to the anus. The perineum supports the outer lingam by swelling and hardening in the same way during erection. Being equally sensitive to stimulation, the re-channeling of sexual energy is engaged only by a momentary and gentle energy-push while exhaling. With this slight input from the index and/or middle finger, the accumulated energy in the 2nd Chakra is redirected. The more these fingers have been "filled" with consciousness, the more effective this practice can be. Which partner applies the energy-input may depend on the ease of access and the ongoing love motions.

➢ **The Scrotum-Pull**
For the scrotum pull, focus on the base area of the testicles where sac and lingam meet. Depending on the anatomy of his 2nd Chakra, your hand may have to envelope his testicles in order to place your finger-tips around the scrotum's base. To re-channel the energy-current, gently pull down on this base for an instant, being careful not to hurt his sensitive testicles.

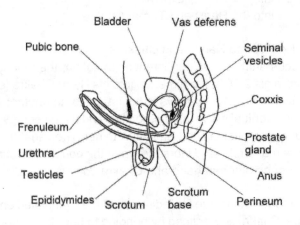

Male "Sacral Plexus"

➢ **The Frenulum Squeeze**
The frenulum is located just underneath the head of the penis. Its tissue - like the mouth's frenulum - is a highly charged receptor for

sexual energy. With a slight squeeze of it, the desire for ejaculation is calmed down, since the energy is redirected.

If the man slowly inhales during the energy application of these external practices, the re-channeling of energy is more effective.

Energy-Fluidity in the Body

Using your mind, along with breathing and visualizations, lets you open the energy-channels. This enables the body to maintain a fluid energy state, which in and of itself is an excellent basis for health. The kernel of every sickness is found in an imbalance of the body, originated by blocked energy.

In a love-encounter, stimulating one particular spot too long, and too physically, may quickly cause an inner rejection. The over-stimulation desensitizes that specific area, easily leading to a short circuit of the energy and blocking it. Since life itself is in constant movement, playing in the field of pleasure and ecstasy naturally entails flexibility of motion and changes of positions.

In case of an energy-block in your lover, which hinders a deeper level of love-expression, don't keep trying hard - in a one-sided attempt - to loosen it. All you can achieve with your determination is the opposite effect: the energy block gets more stubborn.

The energy will flow in its own time. Psychological comfort may offer an environment that allows your partner to unblock through lack of fear. The field of expression can only be unrestricted if both partners have gained freedom from the desire to control. Simply relaxing Spoon Fashion, or lying down in the Butterfly Position, as described above, may give you the needed comfort. Sitting in the Lotus-position in front of each other, and starting to breathe profoundly while gazing into each others eyes may also help unblock the energy. A dance, in which each partner just moves to the rhythm of the music in their own harmony, can loosen up the blocks little by little, or all at once. A squatting tug-of-peace can playfully loosen the energy.

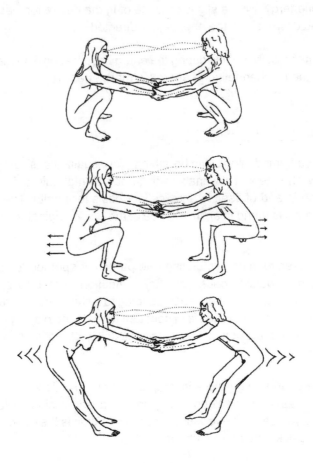

Squatting "Tug-of-Peace"

In a mutual growth situation, the lovers may agree to seek one another's experience, and enhance personal freedom through the increased fluidity of energy. Conscious help in the energetic unblocking of your partner can be accomplished by using the polarity of your hands.

Start by placing your negatively poled hand on your Center Chakra or Heart Chakra. The palm of your positively poled hand is now placed on the blocked body-part of your lover. During strong inhalation the negatively poled hand draws vital energy from your Chakra. Holding your breath, guide this energy up your arm and across your shoulders into your positively poled hand. Exhaling, transmit it into the blocked area of your partner. In this way, a minor block can be dispersed.

If the block you want to work on is dense, it is appropriate to use the energy-poles of your hands in the reversed manner. With the negatively poled hand, energy gets pulled out of the block, induced by your inhalation. Since there is a certain risk of getting stuck with this absorbed energy, serious consideration needs to be given to the exhalation of it. If a long conscious exhalation doesn't completely expel it, a short purification rite is in order. For example, pouring water down your upper arm - with intent - will wash away the absorbed energy.

Healthy love-expression is based on mutual benevolence. The love-encounter is a playful energy-exchange of giving and receiving, harvesting energy and beauty. Starting out with aspirations of getting or even taking is a sure way to receive sickness instead.

Giving (yang) and receiving (yin) intertwine energetically. This interplay is necessary to develop balance and energy-fluidity in the individual. It leads to longevity.

In love-expression the balance of yang and yin is of great importance.

Kisses, touches and movements

which are	most soft and gentle	are yin
	most firm and strong	are yang
	passive and receiving	are yin
	active and giving	are yang

In an ejaculation, the man lets go of yang-energy. In a love-ecstasy, penetrating a woman, he transmits released yang-energy to her 2nd Chakra. He becomes more yin now, while she, being outwardly poled yin in the Sexual Chakra, draws in this yang energy. Whether she is with a man or not, her orgasmic release always lightens her and activates her with yang energy.

Female orgasm and male ejaculation support the balancing of yin and yang in both men and women. Being open to this natural energetic exchange is essential if you seek to develop balance and enrich your growth towards existence as a microcosm.

Since blood is an electrolyte, it is fundamental to the energy-circuit in the body. The practical use of pillows and blankets to assure comfort is at times required to avoid a hindrance of blood-circulation.

For your own sakes, don't become observing and methodical during your love-encounters by following instructions to the letter. Straining to get it "right" can stand in the way of the creative liberty lived by "just-being" and "just-feeling". There is no need to restrict your energy-flow. Trust your body and its wisdom. The body's own wisdom will naturally come to the fore in a beautiful situation that is dealt with from an open mind.

Love Dynamics

Looking at the walls of ancient Indian temples, most Westerners can't believe that the complex postures of ecstasy, depicted there, are achievable with the human body. Their conditioning to stiffness makes this physical flexibility seem exaggerated. However ecstasy, with freedom from energy-blockages, allows movements and motions to blossom in innumerable ways.

An endless variety of pelvic movements exist for both lingam and yoni. A few of them will be described in this book, but only to enhance your own creativity. In this context, bear in mind that every body is different: **a unique creation**.

The Kama Sutra classified couples according to the size of the lingam and the depth of the yoni. Three equal unions between those of "corresponding physical dimensions" were enumerated. It took the sizes of penis and vagina into consideration, for instance: large penis and deep vagina. These, small, medium and large designations also made for six unequal unions with "non-corresponding physical dimensions", for instance: large penis and short vagina or short penis and deep vagina.[75]

In a group of people practicing Hatha-Yoga, comparisons of physical ability in the practice of certain positions are unjust. One person may have a longer back and shorter arms, which allows them do a certain asana very well, whereas other positions, which may be easy for someone else, require tremendous effort from that person. It all comes down to a difference of body dimensions.

Similarly, when expressing love with the physical body, certain positions you enjoyed with a former lover are probably not feasible with your present

---

[75] in Kama Sutra, page 31

partner. Together, you may now delve into an unfamiliar territory, which brings you both a wealth of pleasure.

Nonlinear motions mingled with a variation of positions usually entice more pleasure than simple linear movements.

Round, circular pelvic movements help a woman's partner with ejaculatory control.

Inspiration, bestowed on the man to "let your lingam dance" in the pleasure field of heaven, may increase the experience of beauty for both lovers, more so, when the woman joins the dance with her pelvic motions.

Entering the vagina brings the lingam to internal closeness with the heart of the woman. This has a deep psychological impact on his lover and is closely tied to her feelings of intimacy. The characteristics of the yoni are more yin at its inlet and get progressively more yang as one nears the uterus. In the primal design the yoni, being a microcosm of the woman, embodied the balance of yin and yang within it. However, balance does not entail static functions. Therefore, as a symbol of the microcosm, these yin and yang roles ascribed to the vagina lose significance. Nonetheless, vaginal sensations vary greatly according to the changing depth of the penis.

The angles of entry, as well as the angles of egress, are of great importance. For instance, gliding the lingam along the clitoris at different speeds when entering the yoni, affords the woman a very special feeling.

Speed of movement and alternating from most yin (non-movement) to most yang (thrust), plays an important role in love dynamics. There is also a kind of dynamic in still movement, sending out or receiving energy through the use of conscious breathing, thought-forms and visualizations. The lingam taut on her sacred spot can cause an inner energy-vibration, which invokes more love-magic.

The woman's variation of speed, intensity and timing in the movement of her yoni's ring-muscles can become very important in the love-encounter. The tension and relaxation of the man's Pc-Muscle is just as pivotal.

Novel dynamics are the drumbeat of a rhythmic love-dance.

Front-to-Front Dynamics

The woman on top of him who is laying on his back, at first the couple is calmly breathing together. She starts to move her body after a while, or even just her breasts, caressing his entire body. Slithering her body over him at varying speeds, she can pause in her rhythm and place his penis between her breasts, caressing his Sexual Chakra with them. She can also fondle his Throat Chakra with her breasts. This Chakra is often more restricted in men than women and may need this special attention to open up. As a fringe benefit of this sensual feathering, the conscious awareness of her breasts heightens - inhibiting cancerous growth.

Shakti Dynamic with openness to the universe

This rhythmic caress may entice his lingam into her yoni. She can then open her upper body to the universe in one of the many Shakti Dynamics.

He may raise his upper body, which allows intense eye contact. Breathing together or reciprocally, they can start into new variations and deepen their love-magic with increasing mutual discovery.

Shakti in Calm Erotic

She may sit on top of him with calm erotic sensations, or "Ride the Horse".

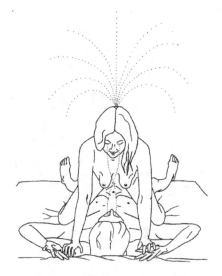

Shakti, "Riding the Horse"

At certain points, this might induce the "Unity-Position". Just be cautious, since not all body-structures freely allow this dynamic. A somewhat blocked 2nd Chakra in the man can also make him feel actual pain in this dynamic.

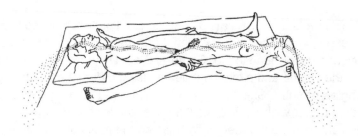

Unity Dynamic

The "Unity Dynamic" can progress into the "Yab-Yum" Dynamic, which may be used to align the Chakras of the partners. A deepening of the experiences in the Yab-Yum is put forth in the next chapter, which describes in more detail the higher universal perception and awareness of consciously forming the "Infinite Circle" in this dynamic.

Yab-Yum Dynamic
with aligned Chakras

The Yab-Yum Dynamic allows circling, rocking, bouncing, back and forth, and up and down movements. Without a doubt it can be used for an intense meditation together, using the Chakras and the enhanced nadi of the Inner Flute.

This dynamic is dependent on the weight of the two partners. In case the woman is much heavier than the man, place a pillow underneath his buttocks to assure comfort.

When he is lying on top of her, he can lightly rub his body across hers, caressing her entire body, until both meander into other motions. This might naturally lead to the "Come-and-Go Dynamic", him penetrating deep in the vagina and almost out again, using different speeds, rhythms and angles of entry. She can grasp his hips, and guide his movements according to her wishes. She may choose to alter this dynamic by lifting her legs and holding her feet, or by bringing the soles of her feet together behind his back in a variation of the Namaste salutation.

He might squat, sit or kneel, his penis penetrating her, while her feet are either on his chest, over his shoulders, or in the air. That way his lingam's highly sensitive head can stroke her sacred spot freely. While she moves her pelvis, he can alter the depth of penetration. They can compose a beautiful stimulating rhythm in a number of front-to-front dynamics.

Yab-Yum Dynamic
with Infinite Circle

In any front-to-front dynamics with all their possible variations, the lovers can bond with each other by being conscious within themselves. As each partner breathes deeply and perceives the melding vibrations, the profound Selves of the lovers are brought together. With no words building between them, the nonverbal communication can be very intense. A feeling of expanded communication, a deeper joining and understanding for each other as they take the earthly path, arises. Spontaneously, the lovers may go into a highly internal love-meditation.

Front-to-Back Dynamics

The man positioned on top of her, while lying on her stomach, she can receive the caresses of his entire body as it glides over her.

Our natural pattern is to hunker down when faced with adversity. This response is meant to protect our vulnerable frontal organs, but if constantly instigated through stress, it often leads to a persistent tightness in the "shielding back".

New situations that are tied to fears of the unknown, or repression, manifest physically in the back - even in those of us who are not attentive to this hidden harm.

Any caressing of this often "heavily burdened" back is welcomed, and always entails a certain degree of healing.

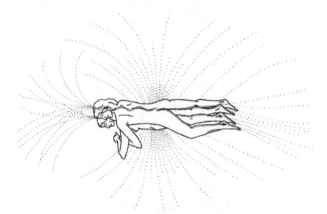

"Hiding in the Canyon"

Loosening her protective shield by his bodily caressing is a gentle opening into the "Hiding in the Canyon" Dynamic. Weaving this magic may awaken her desire to rise back into the "Riding the Tiger".

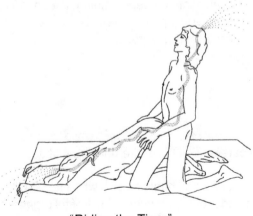

"Riding the Tiger"

Her lying on his back is a love-dynamic, which is not often considered. This overriding position can stimulate her, as well as her lover. Letting her breasts warmly caress him is only one way to reap pleasure from this dynamic. There are a myriad of body parts that can gently stroke the male back, buttocks and legs. Ignoring this possibility - since it relegates the man to a yin position - is only one aspect of the patriarchal background "woven" into the tissue of our psyches.

If he permits her to impregnate his defenses - by allowing her to pamper him with her tender front side - the tenseness of his back can give way to a gratifying looseness. Surrendering this way has nothing to do with passivity or fatalism. There is inner effort involved in letting go, and letting things happen.

Sidewise Dynamics

Front-to-Front

The two lovers can approach each other in a variety of ways, in this relaxed form of attentiveness. Caressing each other with a feather is one way to find and stimulate sensitive body-parts. At first, many people with high levels of stress cannot endure such delicate sensations. Others are simply ticklish, having learned to repress orgasmic feelings. These situations call for patience and creative beginnings, like gently blowing your breath over your lover's body - even from a distance. Other times just resting for a while may deepen the encounter. Facing each other in this way, the partners can build confidence through profound eye contact.

Back-to-Back

Many of us have a tendency to think of this position as a way to reject, or perceive rejection from the turning away of their lover. As a matter of deep encounter, the Back-to-Back Dynamic can offer a wonderful opening to the finer energy exchange of the couple. Having reached synergy, the lovers can well employ this dynamic to stimulate each other's Chakras - and their natural sensibility in the back. Activated Chakras on the backside of the body sensitize perception. However, highly sensitive perception is not to be mistaken for increased vulnerability. Rather, extended consciousness correlates to intense body-perception. For instance, lies can be sensed immediately by the physical energy perception of spoken words. Body perception even alerts you to dangerous vibrations as they appear in the background, or are focused on your body. This lets you walk securely on earth during the Age of Darkness, when lies and brutality are so rampant. Yet, this widened perception may force you to walk your own talk.

Feeling your lover's vibrations of strength and warmth emanating through your back can serve to awaken your subtle perceptions; intense breathing can enhance the spine tingling effect.

Midnight had passed more than an hour ago, when I stepped off the last subway from downtown. To get home, I had to walk through a long, poorly lit tunnel that ran under all the railway tracks, which eventually led into Munich's Hauptbahnhof.

The cold winter's night had obviously kept people from making late-night excursions. Only myself, and one other passenger who had disembarked, started down that tunnel. I could feel this man walking behind me, gradually increasing his pace. The strange shivering I sensed on my back, particularly at the height of my Center Chakra, removed any remaining doubts about his intentions. This man was focused on me and especially my body. The type of vibrations I perceived from him intensified - until they got so dense, that I became aware of a pressing fact. "I have to act - for my protection" was a sudden clear thought. Without regard for the consequences, I stopped walking and slowly turned around. He only needed to take a couple of steps to close in. At this range, I saw that he was obviously a foreigner from a southern country who worked in Germany. He seemed to be startled by my having turned, and was taken aback even more when I greeted him. Pausing for a moment, he answered in German. Realizing that there was no severe language barrier, I told him that I had felt his vibrations. With sudden compassion for his situation, I also told him that I could understand how terribly lonely he could be, as a foreign worker in this big city. He whole-heartedly agreed. This started to diffuse the tension. His honest reply removed any remaining fear. Perceiving his need for social interaction, I invited him for a late night cup of tea in my tiny apartment.

*The ten-minute walk to my home brought out parts of his story as a young and single Turkish worker in Germany. While sipping tea in the warmth of my apartment, he shared with me his desire to be physically close, but since I had not expressed any willingness, he would **now** totally respect me, and never do anything against my wishes.*

Back Embrace

This embrace, commonly referred to as the "Spoon-Fashion Position" can be used in a variety of modes, such as the "Nurturing Dynamic"[76]. One alteration of this dynamic is a sideways version of "Hiding in the Canyon". At other times, it may be welcome as a relaxing interlude between the cresting waves of the love-encounter.

With the woman embracing his backside, she may for instance picture her breasts as unfolding flower buds that blossom while she is exhaling. Her flowering breasts convey a radiation of love energy into his back.

The neck and shoulders are often in dire need of caressing, since the prevailing separation of mind and body, so many of us suffer from manifests there. The Back Embrace provides a comfortable starting point for this healing-dynamic.

Inter-legging

In the sideways variation of Inter-legging, often only the man is on his side, while the woman lays on her back. In this so-called "Scissors Fashion", his lingam can be inside or outside of her yoni.

Sidewise Inter-legging

---

[76] see page 80

This inter-legging may become a momentary resting position. In the dynamic phases of inter-legging, all the different levels of emotional, spiritual and physical energy connections can be felt.

Inter-legging is a many faceted dynamic, but the Sidewise Dynamic of it has fewer variations available simply because of male and female body dimensions.

Common sense calls for the assistance of hands, arms, elbows, forearms, knees and feet, besides pillows and blankets placed to alleviate muscle strain. Dynamic shifts allow for a deeper experience of pleasure and help to avoid tiredness in specific parts of the body. While shifting dynamics, the lingam doesn't need to leave the yoni, close contact can be kept up while changing positions. You both might discover the joy of slightly pushing and pressing the pelvises together, as you flow into the next dynamic.

A person, who allows themselves full pleasure within their own movements, experiences higher orgasmic levels. Only authentic movements based on sensual cognition can lead to a speechless but profound communication with the lover.

If achieving orgasm and ejaculation is not the pre-eminent goal of bodily movements, the couple can experience energetic penetration, orgasm and union. This psychic and energetic exchange can implement Tantra as a way of life.

TANTRIC HIGH UNION ("MAITHUNA")

Reaching the full ecstasy of Maithuna opens one to infinity. You can no longer lose yourself in your "other half", after all, you are "all one", just as any partner you seek is "all one". Individually you are one, a microcosm within yourself, but part of the universal One. Deep within you there is a knowing, that blood either green[77] or red, binds the beings of this earth together. You also know, that this earth is a microcosmic organism in the One macrocosm: the universe.

Having rediscovered this knowing, the search for explanations about the beginning or the end of the universe is no longer of any importance. Time and space are then clarified as limited dimensions, grappled with by a finite mind that experiences birth and death in a material human body.

The intimate intercourse of love vibrations with a partner is limitless - infinite in its creativity. Certainly we need some inspiration to gently enhance our own creativity, which is unfortunately still at the beginner's level. For too many centuries, physical love-expression has been repressed, the time has come for us to individually free ourselves, so as not to repress others in turn.

Let us have a further look at India, where in the nearly forgotten past love-expression was actually incorporated in religious rituals among the ruling Brahmins.

The original tradition of "Bandhas", which means "to bind the energy", was always understood as a connecting of energetic threads in the universal context. There were bandhas in each love-encounter, and the foremost bandha, was tied at the start of a life-long relationship. Parents of the higher class in early India were educated to a higher level of complex universal understanding; therefore their knowledge and wisdom made them feel competent in choosing a partner for their children. This expertise was backed by a homogenous religious system. Modern India demonstrates

---

[77]   Chlorophyll in plants

some real distortions of this custom, however a few exceptions exist, where some competent choices for arranged marriage are still made. Nevertheless, the tradition that imposes the life-partner on people, even frequently during their childhood, is still widespread. At a time when in India, like elsewhere, many more are equipped with the potential to grow into their existence as a microcosm, naturally the Western "love-marriage" is discussed more ardently. Although the Brahminic caste of ancient India was well aware of the Age of Darkness, and its implications, this knowledge did not exempt India from having to go through this period before coming into the Age of Truth.

To thread the energy of love-encounters, tantrics control the use of muscles associated with the first five Chakras. Through mindfulness, the Chakras get inspired with universal breath and cosmic energy. If specific effects are desired, muscles are used in an isolated way. This can lead to a control of the heart-muscle, even to the extent of influencing heartbeat and blood pressure. This kind of awareness also allows a woman to play her yoni like a multi-stringed instrument - in universal harmony. Advanced bandhas are energy threads connected in a natural way, using meditation, visualization (yantras) and mudras.

Bandhas awaken dormant parts of the brain. They always result from energy circuits, and form new ones. "Mind-blowing" orgasms come forth more readily when a strong bandha is present in a relationship. Such an orgasm sparks lightening in the brain that blows the mind free of old programming. Enabled by a nervous system that has been tremendously sensitized - both in the body and in the nadis of the subtle body - messages of pleasure from the yoni or lingam are transmitted to the brain with a force that displaces fear. This newly gained freedom remains until old fears creep in again, however these fears no longer gain control so easily. A formerly blocked, heavy mind may now experience enduring light-fullness. Obviously the halo originates in the brain's complete light-fullness - with this energy beaming forth, an aura ring of light is visible.

Bandhas are a vehicle for the healing arts on a highly developed level, since they can result in huge shifts of the physical body and the mind. After having experienced a lightening of the brain, the flow of unblocked orgasmic energy can be consciously guided - through the nadis - into diseased parts of the body. By visualizing the inner energy-flow, the healing effect gets intensified, and serious illness can be healed on an energetic and physical level. True energetic awareness also causes changes in the bio-chemical processes of the body. A strengthening of the immune system has even been observed in cases of HIV-infection.

A partner in need of healing has to be temporarily more yin during the love-encounter and, with the support of his or her lover, use this tranquility for internal concentration.

Certain dynamics were prevalent in Brahmin[78] circles. They had the express purpose of reaching out into Higher Reality.

Kneeling at the Gate of Pleasure

This dynamic is also called "Kneeling at the Gate of Heaven".

Scholars who have researched Mayan history[79] seem to frequently become aware of a connection with ancient India. In this context, one can observe that the various sculptures of the "Descending God" at the Mayan ruins in Tulum[80], Yucatán, depict the woman's position in this tantric love-dynamic. The word "Maya" existed in Sanskrit, its meaning "illusion", was originally aligned with positive magic. Over time, it has been altered to describe our material world, which forms a veil of illusion.

In this dynamic the woman is lying on her back with her calves resting on the man's shoulders. He is kneeling and has his lingam in her yoni. Either one can additionally touch her jewel or even her sacred spot. She can also attentively caress a single nipple, and guide this enhanced energy through the nadi that channels from the breast down to her Sexual Chakra.

---

[78]   There is in Sanskrit a linguistic connection between 'Brahmin' and the 'Supreme Consciousness of the Universe', called 'Brahma' who is also the God of Creation, see page 22

[79]   Despite history texts that claim that Cortez found only remnants of the Mayan culture, to this day 11 of the 28 original Mayan languages flourish in Central America. Mayans have a vibrant adhesion to their past, to the extent of now actually reassembling ancient scriptures that were burned by the Spanish in 1521.

[80]   'Tulum' means: 'there, where the sun is born'

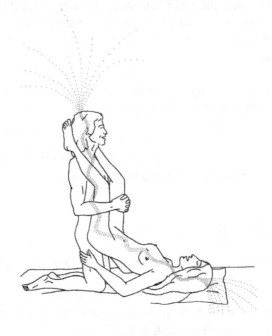

"Kneeling at the Gate of Pleasure"

Cesar, an extraordinary Mexican artist, unified in his person a genetic heritage that included Europe, Africa and Native America.

Having only greeted him a few times in the past, one day I happened upon him as he sat under a thatched roof, transforming a big piece of black coral into a sculpture. I just had to sit down, the tranquility he inspired with the harmonic action of his hands and arms left me spellbound. The background of the coastal surf soothed me, and the peacefulness transported me to a place deep down in the ocean, where that piece of black coral might have come from. I felt myself float off in the infinite ocean, and was so spaced out, that I had the sensation of floating in the universe at the same time. This went on for over an hour. By simply being himself, Cesar had triggered my favorite state of consciousness, which supercedes the limitations of space and time. Intending to thank him, say "good-bye" and disappear, I gratefully gave him a kiss.

Nonetheless, this meeting was not our last and in time our Bandha led to a love-encounter I will never forget. In a large attic-room, equipped with only papaya and water, we fell into an endless love-dance for two nights and a day - rarely interrupted by sporadic sleep. As we once again moved into *"Kneeling at the Gate of Pleasure"*, my inner vision presented me with the outline of stone reliefs, depicted on a number of ruins in Tulum.

"That's the 'Descending God' of Tulum!", I blurted out. My enthusiasm was a puzzle to Cesar, who had never been to Tulum, or heard of these "Descending God" reliefs.

I felt privileged and humbled at the same time, and oh so grateful to the universe.

Partners unified in *Maithuna*, feeling the opening of their Chakras, can clarify their perception of cosmic vibrations and tune into a higher Reality. Their inner eye may suddenly be looking at clear pictures of places, times and alternate dimensions, they have never been aware of.

Mayan "cosmology" was obviously familiar with this and other kinds of tantric practice. Ten years of life, spent mostly in the Mayan region of Mexico, have convinced me beyond a shadow of a doubt that the ancient Mayan ruling class was well aware of how energetic *bandhas* weave throughout the universe. This hypothesis was developed during the giving of numerous healing treatments, which afforded many visions about the Mayan culture at its highpoint, and subsequent decline. Living in full intimacy with the present day culture, as well as with several Maya men, elucidated these visions, which melded into an overview through recurrent meditations.

Three Pointed Pleasure

The woman is in a catlike posture, straddling her lover, who is lying on his back. She may choose to rest her breasts against his chest. He may now energetically awaken her anus with his index finger while either partner touches the jewel. She will enjoy the natural build-up of erotic energy, since in this dynamic the lingam exerts a slight pressure on her sacred spot.

Taking this dynamic a further step, he inserts his finger in the anus, indirectly applying pressure to his lingam - directing its movements for enhanced stimulation of her G-spot. With his other finger lying on her clitoris he applies sensitive animation either with a slight rhythm or through energy beamed from a serene fingertip. A touch from him, that solely moves energy, furthers the stimulation of energy-flow in her nadis. With awareness and exhalation, she can "beam out" this energy into her aura, expand it and send it wherever she chooses. Stimulated this way, the woman senses a highly energetic charge to those zones, which can ignite her Shakti - causing an absolute openness towards the universe.

Be careful not to cross the fine line between ecstasy and over-stimulation in this three pointed dynamic.

Heart-Loving

The partners embrace closely in the Yab-Yum Dynamic. Breathing reciprocally, they charge energetically.

Together they now visualize drawing the energy up into the heart or Heart Chakra. With a long inhalation she pulls the energy up from his lingam into her heart, filling it with his strong yang-energy. Then she exhales - transmitting this enhanced and more powerful energy from her heart into his heart - in an even closer embrace. With a reciprocal intake of breath, he draws it directly into his heart.

Men's hearts are by nature yin. Her empowered yang-energy of the heart or Heart Chakra invigorates his heart through this love-dynamic. By following this tantric energy path, his heart is actually regenerated and healed by his own sexual energy flowing back from his lover.

To a certain degree, the woman's mindfulness, in regard to her feelings and actions, determines whether a man can open his yin heart, and live intimacy to the full extent of Maithuna. Of course, open communication is preferable for intimacy, but a woman can use this technique discretely, without him realizing it.

Yab-Yum Dynamic with an Infinite Circle

Comfortable in the Yab-Yum Dynamic, both lovers can breath reciprocally while slightly swinging their pelvises. Drawing in her breath, she sways her pelvis to the back and up in a rocking motion. Simultaneously exhaling, he moves his pelvis forward and down. The lovers alternate their motions, always however, correlating intake of breath with a drawing motion, while exhaling is associated with letting go and transmitting.

Swinging both pelvises in Yab-Yum Dynamic

Swinging the pelvis individually

During his inhalation he transmits energy to her from his forward moving 2nd Chakra. Taking a deep breath, she draws this energy up into her body, guiding it through her Inner Flute. With her next exhalation, she lets her pelvis descend while transmitting this energy to him from mouth to mouth. According to their focus, she can instead choose to re-transmit this energy from any one of the five higher Chakras.

Energy transmission between the partners can eventually start out at the Crown-Chakra with the help of an energy arch. It can also be sent forth through the Third Eye. Enriching the received energy through focus and inner visualizations of cosmic sources fortifies the energy and its flow. Having reached the 2nd Chakra, this flow can now be directed to the lover while exhaling. Each energy-cycle increases the energy level and excitement.

After a while, the direction of the energy-circle can be reversed; she may transmit energy from her Sexual Chakra into his genitals. With his inhalation, he absorbs this energy from her, drawing it up from his lingam, through all the Chakras of his Inner Flute. He can begin to re-transmit this energy mouth on mouth. Filled with inner vision, he can also exhale while transmitting this energy to her with his Third Eye. When he transmits to her across his universal connection, the Crown Chakra, the feeling and perception of the infinite circle is widened. While receiving this energy through her Crown Chakra, the cosmic *Bandha* circuit is brought into

Yab-Yum Dynamic
with Infinite Circle
(Version 2)

play - as her universal connection swirls into the flow. Her extended inhalation brings the energy down her Inner Flute. This passage allows her to amplify the energy with the focused input of her Chakras, continuing the cycle of energy as it flows to him via the Sexual Chakras.

Advanced practitioners of Tantra in a meditative Yab-Yum Dynamic can open up to the universe through the universal center in the body (navel).

Yab-Yum Dynamic
with openness towards the universe
(Red Tantra)

Having cultivated energy in this way, the beloved ones may feel such a powerful connection to the universal love-vibration, that they are able to send forth energy in the form of Red Tantra[81]. The spiritual voltage of a *Bandha,* and the conscious perception of it, correlate directly with the level of Red Tantra a couple sets in motion.

Life-experiences have let me glimpse the enormous hidden capacity of human beings; I have yet to fathom how far an aware perception of the universe can take us.

---

[81]　see page 2

Trying "hard" to make this or anything happen in life often harvests failure and disappointment. Everything in life has a right time and a right space. The right partner(s) for these kinds of profound universal encounters will appear at the right time. If you are single, or with a lover who chooses not to partake in this kind of experience, you may in the meantime prepare your conscious awareness, as well as your physical body.

Extreme caution is necessary if you desire to enter the path of Tantra with a lover. Do not attempt to manipulate your present partner into these disciplines. Stimulation is a far cry from manipulation, although sometimes the line between them is fine and almost unnoticeable. A partner utilized in this manner, will eventually break out in rebellion or passive resistance that will be unexpected and very difficult to deal with.

Tower Bathed in Light

Tantrics experience the lingam as a microcosm of the body. This is analogous to the logical underpinnings of reflexology, which considers the feet as a microcosm of the whole organism.

In this dynamic, she visualizes her yoni as a sort of tunnel with ringed levels, the light of the sun penetrates between these rings to reach the lingam. This energy-massage of the "tower" (lingam) in her yoni heightens the degree of intimacy for her lover. She can add a physical component to this internal massage by contracting her ring muscles. Picturing herself in a sunlit meadow for instance, she can draw in the energy of the sun while inhaling. Absorbing the light and warmth of this sun through her Third Eye, she can guide it through her Inner Flute into her 2nd Chakra. She now opens the space between the rings of her vagina, beaming this light and warmth to her lover's lingam.

The "Symphony of Love"

With good Pc-Muscle control, she can play with the different ring muscles in her yoni. This way she can compose a harmonic "Symphony of Love" with creative key and chord changes followed by refrains and fluctuations of rhythm. This joyful music making can easily lead the couple into a "Symphony of Universal Harmony". The innermost ring-muscles of the yoni are progressively sensitive; their contraction pulls the energy to her upper body. Naturally, her yoni is like the lingam, a microcosm of her body.

Samdamsaja ("The Tongs")

This "internal embrace" is a variation of the Tower Bathed in Light. The woman pulls the lingam or "tower" deeper and deeper into her yoni with strong contractions of her love-muscle. Every inhalation is accompanied by a contraction. At the ultimate peak of contractions, she squeezes the lingam as close to her heart as possible, while holding her breath as long as she can. Excited by her inner contractive movements, her Shakti-energy may explode and bathe his lingam. Simultaneously, in a long exhalation she releases the muscle contractions in her yoni. He may inhale and draw the Shakti-energy up into his highest Chakras, using it for visions and universal energy-connections.

Pulsing

The woman's Pc-muscle squeezes the lingam with increasing speed. In between the soft clenches she relaxes her yoni totally when exhaling. The faster the change from squeeze to release, the faster her breathing becomes. If the man's love-muscle is well trained, his lingam naturally taps out the rhythm on her sacred spot. An ultimately long squeeze and release can be an ecstatic introduction to an advanced energy dynamic.

Shakti Dynamics

Spiritual ecstasy is a strong component of the "Shakti" Dynamics. [82]

The Circle Dance of Shakti

The woman places herself, sitting upright on her lover. She can use a variety of ways to awaken her Shakti energy with the energy of the lingam, which her lover has offered by laying on his back. Moving her pelvis in circles, she playfully enjoys the changes of

---

[82] see diagrams from page 112 on

rhythm and depth, while lifting and lowering herself. In varying the lingam's angles of entry and egress in her yoni, she builds her own ecstasy; and eventually she lowers herself one last time – slowly and naturally – releasing her Shakti. Feeling individual and universal unity, enhanced by inner visualizations, makes this rhythmic dance a wonderful physical sensation. He feels this intimate flowing in the universe - actively offering his lingam to this cosmic twirl from his more yin-position.

He may place his hand(s) on her heart or his own heart. Other times, he can integrate the principles of polarity in the Namaste hand-position. He also can choose to connect the energy between her heart and Third Eye by putting his positively poled hand[83] on her heart and placing his negatively poled hand gently on her forehead. Using the natural polarity push and pull between his hands, he can now enhance the inner flow of her heart energy into her Visionary Eye. Do not exert pressure on her forehead with your receiving hand: this may very quickly accumulate energy around her Third Eye and result in tension or even severe headache.

Shakti's Cobra

Lying stretched out over him, she feels his lingam in her yoni. Placing her hands beside her lover's shoulders, she slowly raises her upper body as if moving into the Cobra asana of Hatha Yoga. While she is arching towards the sky, the awareness of connecting her body to the universe may emerge through a specific inner vision. During her unhurried upward stretch, both can focus on the energy threads between the four Chakras, which integrate their center, heart, speech and vision. These energy-beams, in being pulled and getting longer, offer a couple many possibilities for experiencing their bodies as a tool of spiritual interconnectedness.

Depending on the condition of her lower back, the lovers may take each other's hands letting them dance energetically together in the air. At this point, their physical link is maintained by their hands as well as their legs and hips.

---

[83]   usually the right hand, see page 6

Shakti's Flight

Well-trained practitioners of Tantra can give wings to Shakti's Cobra. Starting out in the Cobra dynamic, they now join hands and raise them to support her coming flight. Bringing his strong hamstrings and Pc-Muscle-group into play, he supports her pelvis, so that she can now also lift her legs. The physical support for this advanced dynamic is only provided through the hands and the lingam - yoni bond. The sensation of free flight gives her mind the liberty to travel wherever her heart and spirit desire.

With an intake of breath, she can guide the energy of her flight from her 7th and/ or 6th Chakra through her Inner Flute down into her vagina. Now exhaling, she transfers this energy filled with vision and universal knowledge to him via his lingam. Reciprocally breathing, he receives this refined and potent energy during his inhalation. Extending his inhalation, he raises this energy up through his Kundalini channel (= Inner Flute). By permitting the naïveté of his free inner child, he may after a while be able to envision these images of the universe along with his lover. Within a firm bandha connection, he may be able to expand these visions. If both partners have yet to understand the significance of these insights, situations in life that are connected to them will often appear in the not too distant future. Being alert to these occurrences will grant clear comprehension.

When still caught in a heavy psychodrama from childhood or from a former lifetime, emotional obstacles will not allow such a full experience of the tantric way. This kind of psychological framework pollutes the interpretation of these images from the universe.

Once, during our many years of long-distance relationship - labeled as a "mystical marriage" by a woman from New York - my "mystical" husband Vaseles sent me one of his collages. It depicted a man flying in the streets of New York. This work of art spoke to me, although I was not always predisposed to the style of art that Vaseles expressed.

Years later, in our sanctuary underneath the almost pyramid-like roof of our Highland Avenue home in Jersey City, I was reminded of this collage. Being held only by his hands and penis, I was flying through space. There was no strain; my body was in a loose, relaxed form of a cross as his Pc-Muscle anchored my lower body to the earth. Yet, I was floating through spaces and dimensions at will, observing and understanding the weaving of several cosmic bandhas.

Vaseles and I never experienced the transmission of these visions, since our energy vibrated on differing frequencies.

The life force, unfolding through the orgasmic explosion, is full of magic and highly transformational. In Tantra, nothing is considered more profound than the psychic and spiritual climax experienced in a peak of physical ecstasy.

The woman, who becomes aware of being as wide and open as the universe, is a natural channel for the rebirth of cosmic love-vibrations on earth. United as spirits, in the perception of our deepest and highest physical feelings, our consciousness "expands into the beyond". This love-connection with the universe empowers. It provides us with a knowing wisdom about being part of the One, "Great Spirit" or "God and Goddess". With this wise knowledge, an individual can consciously mold his or her life, being aware of her or his own existence as a co-creator for all creation.

The augmented energy, originally freed up and drawn on by the two lovers, can be directed internally or externally to wherever their minds decide. This gift of love can be shared so expansively, that most people can't even dream of the possibilities. It can, for instance, be sent out vibrationally to the universal family, so that one day, our family will find a true loving way to live together on this planet earth. You are the healer, creator and constructor of the reality of your own life, as well as the human world.

This sex magic is called Red Tantra. We are in need of this transformational love to heal ourselves, and our planet.

THE BASE CHAKRA CONNECTION

You have surely experienced multiple positions and movements, which are not described in this book. As lovers, you have probably figured out that when the pelvises are pushed and stroked against each other, the clitoris receives wonderful stimulation through the man's pubic bone and hair, if not removed.

Your explorations as a couple may have led you to discover exceptional intertwining dynamics, which are made exclusively available by the uniqueness of your particular body structures.

Considering how we were socialized in the Western world, at one point you might have still felt a slight resistance to certain avenues of experience. Participating in a love-encounter, you might have tried to "jump over a canyon", when you weren't yet sure whether you felt psychologically ready for the event. One of the most delicate steps is the Stimulation of the Base Chakra.

In the tantric tradition, so-called anal sex requires a ritual bath, towels, pillows and blankets, to assure tactile comfort. Rough fingernails need to be trimmed, and the use of a water-soluble lubricant is strongly recommended. Oil based creams and lotions do provide good lubrication, however they may affect the function of the intestines. During or after the Base Chakra connection, health-consciousness shouldn't be ignored: wash the lingam or the finger, which has entered the anus, before touching the yoni with it.

The Base Chakra stimulation needs to be started slowly, especially if this is a new field of encounter for the lovers. In a subtle tender massage of the anus, you will find out how you and your partner feel about a further exploration of this avenue. Eye and heart-contact, with profound breathing, is very important to partners having anal sex. A gentle rhythmic massage in the area of the 1st Chakra - where we have a strong energy-connection with the center of the earth - can be combined with conscious breathing and inner visualizations to help awaken the Kundalini. Allowing this massage without any inner reservations relieves chronic stress and strain as tensions leave the body. Tender Base Chakra stimulation can lead to a very natural relaxation. This primal release allows a loosening of energy blockages in the body, to a degree never imagined.

A gently touching massage of the prostate gland, along with consciously fingering the hidden part of the lingam that is near the anus, can lead to an extraordinarily orgasmic experience for the man during his Base Chakra stimulation.

It might be very necessary that you talk openly together before the lingam enters her or his[84] anus for the first time. The foreplay needs a gentle stimulation and the use of lubrication. The thickness of his lingam and the formation of her or his buttocks may require more preparation by the use of pillows etc.

Facing each other particularly during a Base Chakra connection is recommended in Tantra. Mounting a woman from behind can easily trigger resistance, due to her apprehension of animalistic tendencies. Eye and soul contact can be secured by using the dynamic of "Kneeling at the Gate of Pleasure" and its variations.

Until she or he feels completely comfortable with the penetration, the partner should remain motionless, or with almost no movement. An energetic fountain might flow through his lingam, and is felt by his lover, sometimes even as a slight physical motion. The pelvic movements of the penetrated partner allow her or him not to cross the threshold of pain. The woman's movement, accompanied by clitoral stimulation done by either partner, brings her increased excitement, until she reacts to this pleasure by sharing it with her partner through conscious movement of the anal ring-muscles.

Treating the Base Chakra connection as "a must in tantric love-expression", would be wrong. The Brahmins knew many ways to express love consciously, and it was always the choice of the couple, even if influenced by their understanding of the cosmic *Bandha* they shared. In ancient India, ignoring or rejecting certain body parts was not an element of society, like it is in the "civilized" world. Some people actually feel disgusted

---

[84] Although not expressly mentioned in surviving tantric texts, homosexuality existed in ancient India, however, it was probably far more exceptional than in today's Western societies.

by their sweat or anything else their own bodies produce naturally. Still more intense is the disgust directed at excrement and the anus it comes from. Our conditioning trained us to disregard this part of the body, denying us the full scope of its high sensitivity.

Repression by its very nature leads to an opposite reaction, and the Base Chakra connection between males has come out into the open. The sexual energy-accrual of exclusively homosexual men and women has not yet been fully understood by me, even though I have experienced a lesbian love-encounter.

Naturally, the man's "G-spot", the prostate gland, can only be reached through entering the anus. Assuming that, like the female G-spot, this sensitive gland is also a storage place of sexual and emotional wounds, it also needs to be freed from this pain.

The deep heart connection of many homosexual couples is easy for me to comprehend, as are the *bandhas* they may have formed during former lifetimes. Yet, as a woman, I can truthfully only discourse on female homosexuality. For myself, the missing element in lesbian love-expression is the tremendous explosion of the Shakti - this endless energy of and for creation - that I can only experience through exchanging vitality with a man. This original life-force, inherent in the intercourse of male and female life-creating organs, is so potent that it can materialize a human being. Personally, I have decided to transform this potential, and use this life giving force for healing. With this source at hand, supporting the healing of paralysis is not a revelation; the life force itself is the miracle.

HAVING REACHED THE PEAK

A woman can release her Shakti-energy in a series of orgasms for many hours. Orgasms usually cause her to be more yang and activate her strength. After an ejaculation the man is more yin, and so is his penis, which is now receptive to the abundant energy in the woman's vagina. Keeping his lingam in the yoni, feeling intimately embraced, with a long inhalation he absorbs the Shakti energy inward and up into his body. After having expended a lot of yang-energy, most men unconsciously take now a kind of long breath, regaining energy. In this way, women and men can gradually facilitate the balance of yin and yang, which is an indispensable step on the path towards unfolding as a microcosm.

Unfortunately, there are women who use their recently stimulated Pc-Muscle to expel an ejaculation-weakened penis from their vagina. These women don't realize the kind of energetic and psychological harm they engender in themselves, as well as in their partner, with this behavior. Even physical damage is done when colder air enters their much warmer yoni too swiftly.

Love-intimacy in a light and luminous milieu wouldn't allow such conduct. Sharing the highest and most profound that is attainable as a human being, gives rise to true caring - without dependency. Self-responsibility is just naturally there.

It then becomes clear, that no situation can really be repeated. Every sharing of life-intimacy is in the "here and now" - a creation of the moment - a surrendering into being.

The love-encounter cannot be held onto - extended artificially by one of the partners, since it is a creation of the two. It can just be felt, enjoyed and appreciated every moment while it is happening.

Love is free
it has to be
it can't be told
it can't be sold

Much less can it be bought. However simple gifts, offered as signs of love, can be freely received. Their quality or quantity does not put either partner into obligation. Obligations start to spin the wheel of guilt, which inexorably grinds down unconditional love. The more unconditional the love the less judgment and expectation. Everything from your lover is a gift, even his or her existence. Observation, subtle perception, and an endless opening up to learning are connected with true love.

I was once in charge of the youth hostel in Grand Canyon Village, Arizona, for several weeks as a vacation-substitute.

On a cold day, with no end to falling snow, the first guest to arrive was quite friendly. This Swiss German and his brother sought shelter after having driven the only car that made it through the snowstorm from Flagstaff. "Volkswagen vans are reliable in every situation," he intoned. They had spent an entire year with it on the roads of South East Asia, arriving less than two weeks previously in the western United States. Their feats of travel were not the only unusual thing about these brothers. That they should be related at all was hard to believe; they were so different in manner, thought and physical build.

I felt a special vibration of great kindness and clear human values coming from him, while I led one of these brothers to a room in our small and usually overfilled building. There where normally up to 25 people of international origin staying in the hostel, and every day brought new surprises. I wondered what this new evening might bring.

The house was in silence that evening, indeed an unusual occurrence.

The three of us sat down to a special meal in front of the fireplace, and enjoyed it in a ritual way with candle light and meditative music. It turned into a special celebration; since our paths had crossed East and West, we felt unified in a whole and holy atmosphere in that first month of the dreaded year 1984.

At midnight, sure that no late stragglers would still be wanting a hostel-bed, we made things more comfortable in front of the fireplace. There were no negative thoughts or vibrations - only three absolutely different souls, enjoying each other's uniqueness in the appreciation of being brought together. Everything was considered a gift, since we had no expectations and simply felt enriched by our differences.

When words became too coarse, we began to tenderly touch each other, uncovering a finer form of communication between us. I let myself go somewhere else, into an unknown realm of existence; my body was like a vessel floating in dimensions out of space and time. Each of them experienced deep joy at seeing his blood brother unified in ecstasy with me, while I drifted in the cosmos. Becoming aware of the circumstances, I suddenly sat up for a moment and, with gratefulness in my heart, these words slipped out of my mouth: "The world is really changing!" I had glimpsed the vision of the Native American story told to me just six months previous:

"At the beginning of the world there were two brothers. They lived together in harmony, sharing everything in life. Whenever one of them saw something beautiful, he brought it to the attention of his brother so as to give to him the joy of also experiencing this beauty. Seeing the sun come out from behind a cloud after a heavy rain, it was pointed out to the brother. If one brother heard the lovely song of a bird, the other brother got made aware of it, too. A beautiful flower was always shown to the brother. The earth's gifts that maintained their material bodies were shared with gratefulness and joy. Because they lived so well in the rapture of peace and harmony, they were granted a special gift. This gift was a woman.

One of the brothers - never thinking to question their way of life - was also intent on sharing this wonderful gift naturally with his brother. The other brother however, began to act in a wanting way for this newest gift, and tried to keep it for himself. This was the way conflict was brought into the world.

The woman gave birth to children conceived by both brothers. The children of the first brother formed the 'snake-tribe', the children of the other brother formed the 'turtle-tribe'."

You cannot be the one who makes someone else truthfully happy. Everyone can achieve happiness only in themselves, by freeing the inner Self.

You can only love in **your** way, and you receive love the only way you can at the moment. Having grown to receive love in a full and comprehensive way allows one to recognize, that often in the past love had been offered by different persons (for instance parents) in a way that had not yet been understood and honored as an expression of love.

A wider understanding will rush through your mind-body-connection, reaching the depths of comprehension, so that all the misunderstandings in our human world can be fathomed, even felt in the bones. Profound forgiveness will take place in a person who has experienced the freedom of the universal energy and its love-vibration. A phase of sadness - about the way we human beings have deformed our original materialization of love - rushes through such a person as well. This sadness is one more reason to practice White and Red Tantra.

This deeply liberating insight has nothing to do with conventional knowledge. It changes one's entire consciousness of oneself, others and the world. The Mexican Yaki tribe calls this "body-wisdom". In the Hindu tradition it's called *jnana*.

Almost totally hidden in the mists of our perception lies the awareness of the "gene to gene" communication that takes place in an intimate relationship. In a cosmically strong *bandha* this information can get filtered little by little into "the awakened state", the consciousness. In such a developed state, not only former lifetimes can come into the open and get clarified. This body wisdom can lead to astral travel across the universe and journeys into the past and future, sometimes even simultaneously.

My three month renovation project of the house I had rented in San Cristóbal de las Casas, Chiapas, was almost finished when one late afternoon my doorbell (a cow's bell) rang. Norbert, a blond Italian from Southern Tyrol stood there, as I opened the door. Our informal repartee had always been comfortable; I had enjoyed the chance to speak in my native Southern Bavarian dialect with him.

"I'll help you, if you don't mind." Being tired of my project, I readily accepted his offer, and answered "OK, I'll make us a nice meal afterwards." When the work was completed, I made our meal.

We feasted in my special room which had the huge mandala painted on the wall. This work of art had initiated the renovation project, and in the meantime had already served as my tunnel for long-distance-healing.

The intestinal affliction, that left my body on the threshold of death some seven years previous, had activated the healer in myself. It had also taught me the significance of relaxed digestion, which is provided by lying on one's side while eating. Reclining on a big mattress on the floor triggers other people into thoughts of "sleep", "sex" and "sickness" so easily, that I rarely shared food with my guests that way.

Painted Mandala
(diameter around 2,5 meters)

With Norbert, it was pleasant to share this repast on the mattress; there had always been a comfortable brother and sister like familiarity between us. Our midnight meal brought out in him a longing for another type of intimacy. His discreet advances awakened in my body the desire to feel the presence of his head on my abdomen, although sexual intentions were not involved.

Even though we had not undressed; with his head comfortably lying on my stomach, I could feel the heartbeat in my clitoris adjust itself to the rhythmic movement of his breast. His deep breathing started a subtle wave of motion through his chest and head, which must have transmitted a surge of energy to me. The discharge of his energy melded with my awareness. Funneling through my 7th Chakra, it shot out of my head like a rocket using the tunnel of my mandala. Immediately I was on Mars. Of their own accord, my legs took me on an endless journey, and slowly I started to notice the surrounding landscape. The sand beneath me was reddish and heavy, and the very few leafless shrubs looked dead, however the juice of life nourished their branches. These life-forms communicated their sentience to me vibrationally, just like plants on earth have done on many occasions. The few small rocks strewn across the reddish sand stood out in their lack of color, somehow lifeless. There was also a pond, strangely, I could smell it as well as see it, and somehow I knew that as wide as it seemed, it was shallow all the way across.

Without consciously experiencing a return to my body, I suddenly felt awfully tired. I was barely aware of the source, as I heard my voice say to Norbert, " I have to go to bed, but you can stay here in this room and sleep, if you want."

While having breakfast the next morning I asked Norbert, "what happened with you, last night?" "Oh, it was the best trip I've ever had in my life" he answered, "I can't believe we weren't stoned". He knew my reputation as a drug-free person.

Six years later, after a decade's absence from Europe, I was back in my hometown of Munich. I enjoyed staying with my elderly mother for that summer. One day she became uncharacteristically persistent, when she again reminded me about the "really interesting space-exhibition" at the German Museum. She managed to convince me that it was a "must see"!

In one corner of the huge exhibition halls, a landscape of Mars had been erected, following the specifications of the images and data sent to earth by an American space mission. How well I knew it! Only here, it's pulsation was almost unnoticeable. The intensity of Martian life-vibration I had felt, while Norbert's head had been lying on me, was much more powerful. It seemed like the huge mandala on the wall, had somehow served as a space-time tunnel. Paradoxically, limited resources at the time in Mexico only allowed me to paint this artwork with the three elementary colors.

Body wisdom was an integral part of the disciplines used to gain knowledge about the universe in the ancient culture of the Mayas. There are no surviving texts from this period, since they were so thoroughly incinerated under the orders of Diego de Landa, the first Spanish Bishop of Yucatán. Later, in the middle of the 16th century, this very bishop proceeded to write the "authoritative" descriptions of the Maya, which are often used as a source by scholars in their attempts to interpret the many hieroglyphs still extant on Mayan ruins. It is very doubtful that these researchers, coming from a base of conventional perceptions, can ever really gain insight into the science of this ancient culture. They do the best they can, however to this day none of them has been able to discern how the Maya were able to construct such an accurate calendar, which can only result from precise knowledge of the solar system. In depth understanding can only be achieved by a person who is free of programming from any culture.

At the core of the 65 tantric sciences lies body wisdom, at the same time it is also the goal of these disciplines. The cosmic aspect was not always explored in the lives of tantric practitioners of ancient India. Yet, the original disciplines of Yoga[85] as well as the philosophies of the Upanishads being taught in a great variety of schools in ancient India, were all based upon this holistic insight into the "nature of things".

This path of wisdom cannot be found by simply following an imposed authority. One's true feelings - **not** those that have been manipulated by a conditioned brain - are the real and honest authority.

A teacher or an illuminative book might seem necessary at the beginning of the journey, in order to tear down taboos and glimpse the gateway of knowledge. As much as some would like to try, it's impossible to copy a master. A teacher can only be loved and respected for being in existence, in his or her own special way. As a matter of fact we are all teachers for each other and students from one another.

"Go however far to find honest joy.
Learn from any who is wise, though a boy."[86]

The Vedas, which have a wide range of theories, share one goal: *moksha*, which means "liberation". Tantra seeks to live *darshana*, the "liberated Self".

---

[85]   Hatha, Raja, Bhakti, Jnana and Karma Yoga

[86]   Panchatantra, page 161/162

THE CREATION OF THE WORLD

INTEGRATED ONENESS

A liberated Self has essential material needs - shelter and clothes - which protect the "temple of the spirit on earth" against inclement weather. Utilizing this physical existence to the fullest can only be accomplished by eating natural food in a healthy way. Spiritual health is engendered in love, and is vitalized by its expression.

Against these basic prerequisites for balanced human life, each of us can bear witness to the extent of the inadequacy of our present world. This lack of harmony started to intensify, when societies sought to expand their territorial domain by imposing their ideologies on others.

However its origins began in mythical times, as humans left the Oneness: "paradise".

Whether we
- ate the apple from the forbidden "tree of knowledge" or
- started out as luminous beings floating at will in the universe or
- have been created by the union of Shakti and Shiva,

we have obviously all somehow separated from the One.

We have even subdivided this one big organism that we live on, into innumerable parts - calling them "mine", "ours" and "yours", separating them with fences and borders, even keeping smaller parts under lock and key. We have even divided ourselves, provoking disease by living duality in our own existence.

Being at the zenith of these separations and divisions, our longing for unification has reached a level of urgency. We are desperately searching for the meaning of life, and want to come home to the oneness we call "God" - the "Supreme Energy of the Universe". Paradoxically, we are already a part of this Great Spirit, we only need to realize it.

We are already tapping into the telepathic connection that exists between all of us, however the majority is not yet aware of this. The term "collective unconscious" is frequently used for this telepathic network, over which the individual Selves are interconnected on certain wavelengths. This network of wills extends globally and universally. God, the Cosmic Will, is the unity of will coming from all the beings in the cosmos. Our planet is only humanity's temporary home in this universe.

Awareness of one's authentic will causes at least a "soupcon" about the cosmic plan to come forward. With this insight, one willingly surrenders to this plan, a natural process impossible to confuse with fatalism. In personally living authentic will, you fulfill your individual spiritual purpose and the cosmic will.

The oneness we originally came from can be clearly distinguished from the oneness we are heading to after this long age of separation.

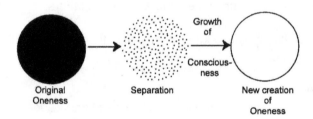

Evolution of Oneness

In this new creation of oneness, there is consciousness about the oneness. In the original oneness, consciousness of the unity did not exist.

Long sojourns all over India, and extraordinary experiences in Pushkar, Rajastan, the site of the only temple ever consecrated to Brahma, the "Creator", eventually led me to surmise this conclusion:

~ According to Hinduism, the universe originated in the union of Shakti and Shiva[87].

---

[87]   see page 30

This obviously represents only the creation of the original Oneness and the philosophical foundation of its separation, the Age of Darkness. No wonder, Shiva[88] the "God of Destruction", has been worshipped for millennia in so many temples throughout India. The myths tell us that Brahma, the "Supreme Consciousness of the Universe", had to become upset with the Hindus before they would even build a single temple, in which to worship Him.

Our present development, characterized by a growth of consciousness, initiates the Age of Truth, a new creation of the universe and human world, which is starting to be originated in the union of Shakti and Brahma. ~

Yet, the tantric way of life was brought to the fore in Hinduism. This well-founded path can give us a guideline for the progression towards the neo-oneness. It shows us possible doorways of communication with the universe, deepening our growth into higher consciousness.

---

[88]   see page 22

TANTRIC TRADITION OF WOMEN TEACHING MEN

Women's capacity for ecstasy and trance is easier to induce. They have natural opportunities to sense the experience of unity in their bodies since they unite in themselves a part of or an entire other entity: a man's penis, a growing child. Therefore, the guidance of knowledgeable wise women in helping men step into the realm of Oneness makes sense. This school of feminine-cosmic-intuition flourished in ancient India and probably also in ancient Tibet.

The Tibetan tradition of Dakinis is traced back to the worship of ancient Indian Goddesses. These earliest known deities of India, called Yoginis, were linked to special places in nature, particular villages or exceptional crossroads. Long before Shiva had, according to the myths, left his original home on Mount Kailasa[89] to arrive in India, these Goddesses resided on their 108 *pithas* (seats) in the "Forest of Bliss". This "forest" – the city of Benares[90] – subsequently became the center of Brahmanism, in which Tantra was cultivated in religious rituals. Those pre-historic Yoginis knew the truth of love; in living this knowledge, they taught men the basics of cosmic love-expression.

In later eras, famous female personalities in the religious field, were also called "Yoginis". They lost their influence when patriarchal thought-forms took the foreground. This began long before India became an English colony.

However, in the sanctuary of Indian temples during the last decade before the year 2000, a very few Yoginis were still providing guidance in tantric love-expression. This teaching aimed at a select group of men is often integrated into rites of Kali-worship. Kali, the Goddess of Death and the Earth, becomes the Goddess Tripurasundari[91] upon transcending her fear of death. Tantric instruction in temples was outlawed by the British and to this day the continuation of these disciplines remains hidden from

---

[89] far North in the Himalayas of Western Tibet
[90] today Varanasi
[91] see page 19

Western eyes.[92] The entrance to these special sanctuaries in a very few temples is - if at all - allowed only to Hindus.[93] Even if a person of Western origin follows the traditional Hindu way of life, the Western body-build cannot be hidden from the discerning eyes of temple gatekeepers.

Presently, during the transition from the Age of Darkness to the Age of Truth, we are in great need of Yoginis and their wisdom about the cosmic truth of love. These women can help us to accept our true material reality: this beautiful physical body – that is material earth energy mingled with spiritual energy from the infinite universe.

Yoginis are indispensable in the challenge to alter the outcome of the following Tibetan creation myth:

"In the past, we were spiritual beings of free-floating energy, weightless and full of light. We nourished ourselves from the rapture around us. Enchanted by our own existence, dancing and intertwining energy to the full, we were in and of infinite beauty.

After endlessly long times, the appetizing earth raised itself out of the waters. It had color, scent and taste. As a natural element of our existence, we started to take pleasure from this earth, absorbing parts of it into our beings. Taking more and more of the earth into our beings, we came to lose some of our joyful luminosity.

When our light-fullness eventually vanished; sun, moon, day and night, weeks and months, seasons and years came forth. We continued to enjoy the tasty earth and started to maintain our newly formed existence from it. Gradually, our free-floating energy had taken on a denser materiality.

After an indefinite span of time, the earth began to grow extensions of itself. Our nature of enjoyment led us to imbibe these parts of the earth as well. The continuous intake of material earth-energy formed us into very solid material bodies, earthen beings.

---

[92] personal information related to me by the Brahmin in Varanasi, who did the worship on me described on page 73. He had been instructed by such a Yogini in the Kali Temple of Calcutta in 1992.

[93] discerned while Hindus tried to smuggle me into the sanctuary in the temple of Madurai

We still enjoyed intertwining our energy, which led to a reproduction of our earth-species. Discovering that this new home was limited, we started to divide the earth into fields, and developed the idea of "mine" and "yours". To separate these divisions, we built fences and borders, and gradually we introduced possessions, ownership, envy and greed until we became totally focused on materiality",[94]

......fighting over our earth, and habitually destroying it by fighting about it.

May this book be put to use in the quest to conclude this history, so that we can live as a light-full and joyful family on this earth.

---

[94] Lama Anagarika Govinda: Grundlagen tibetischer Mystik, loose translation from German edition, page 81

APPENDICES

Appendix 1: YIN and YANG in Foods

This system goes back to the founder of
Macrobiotics, the Japanese doctor
Sagen Ishizuka (1850-1909)

A) YIN and YANG in the Wide Range of Foods

↑ YIN (extension)	refined sugar dairy products sweet, tropical fruits brown sugar honey, maple syrup tomatoes[95] less sweet fruits, grown in colder climates bleached flour greens and veg. with expanding leaves seaweed above ground veg. with dense structures sprouts
YIN and YANG balanced	grains nuts, seeds[96] legumes and soy bean products[97] eggs
↓ YANG (contraction)	root vegetables except beets pork[98] white fish beets[99] chicken, turkey[100] red fish beef[101] meat from goat meat from rabbit or deer meat from buffalo

---

[95] above the ground red vegetables are more YIN than other vegetables
[96] fattier seeds and nuts are more YIN
[97] bigger beans are more YIN
[98] fattier pork incorporates less YANG
[99] red root vegetables are more YANG than other root vegetables
[100] tatty poultry is less YANG, chicken fed with estrogens is less YANG
[101] cattle fed with estrogens is less YANG

B) YIN and YANG in Vegan Nutrition

↑ YIN	refined sugar
(extension)	sweet tropical fruits
	brown sugar
	honey, maple syrup
	tomatoes[102]
	less sweet fruits, grown in colder climates
	bleached flour
	greens and veg. with expanding leaves
	seaweed, spirulina, blue algaes
	above ground veg. with dense structures
	sprouts
YIN and YANG	grains
balanced	nuts, seeds[103]
	legumes and soy bean products[104]
YANG	root vegetables
↓ (contraction)	beets[105]

C) General rules
whatever grows above the soil is YIN
whatever grows under the surface of the soil is YANG
all seeds, grains, nuts and legumes are balanced in YIN and YANG

---

[102] above the ground red vegetables are more YIN than other vegetables
[103] fattier seeds and nuts are more YIN
[104] bigger beans are more YIN
[105] red root vegetables are more YANG than other root vegetables

NATURAL BIRTHCONTROL

1. A woman's montly cycle entails only **10 hours of fertility.**
These occur 12 – 17 days before the 1st day of the next menstruation.

Most commonly, a woman experiences these 10 hours of fertility
14 days before the first day of her next period.

Example, wherein the <u>cycle is 28 days long and the menstruation lasts 5 days</u>:

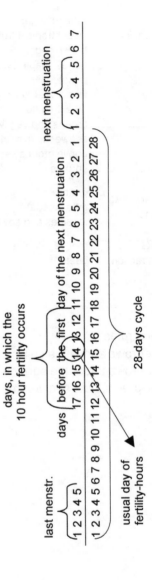

2. Once in the womb of a woman, the man's **sperm** retains its fertilization-capacity for at least 36 hours – to a maximum period of 5 days.

Normal duration of potential fertilization is 2 days

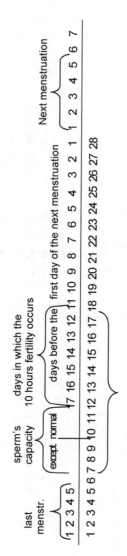

11 days of potential pregnancy

3. Conclusion: In case a woman doesn't sense her fertility-hours and/or hasn't enough experience, she needs to be careful only during these 11 days of her cycle, if she wants to avoid pregnancy.

4. Your own cycle: You can apply this system to your own cycle after having observed the length of your cycle for at least half a year.

Start taking notes after any altering effect of birth-control pills has ceased – they can change the pattern completely.

1 2 3 4 5   17 16 15 14 13 12 11 10 9 8 7 6 5 4 3 2 1 1 2 3 4 5 6 7

1 2 3 4 5 6 7 8 9 10 11 12 13 14 15 16 17 18 19 20 21 22 23 24 25 26 27 28

Bibliography

Ancient Secrets of Kundalini   by   Gopi Krishna,
UBS Publishers,
New Delhi, London, 1995

The Art of Sexual Ecstasy -   by   Margo Annand,
The Path of Sacred Sexuality   Edit. Jeremy P. Tracher Inc.
for Western Lovers   Los Angeles, 1989

The "G" Spot   by   Alice Kahn L, Beverly
Whipple and J.D. Perry,
Holt Rinehart & Winston
New York, 1982

Grundlagen tibetischer Mystik   by   Lama A. Govinda,
(German)   Samuel Wieser,
Germany, 1969

Kama Sutra of Vatsyayana   by   R. Burton, F.F. Arbuthonot,
Diff. Editions,
i.e. Jaico Publ. House
Bombay 17th Impr., 1995

Das Leben als Kosmisches   by   Helmut Uhlig,
Fest - Magische Welt des   Gustav Lübbe Verlag,
Tantrismus (German)   Bergisch Gladbach, 1998

Light on Yoga   by   BKS Iyengar,
Harper Collins Publisher,
India, 1994

The Mayan Factor   by   Jose Argüelles,
Bear and Company,
Santa Fe, New Mexico 1993

The Mind of the Cells   by   Satprem,
Institute for Evolutionary Research,
Mount Vernon,
Washington, 1992

The Panchatantra   transl.   Arthur W. Ryder,
       by   Jaico Publishing House,
Bombay, Delhi, Madras, Bangalore,
17th Impr. 1993

Savitri	by	Sri Aurobindo Sri Aurobindo Ashram Trust, Pondicherry, India, 1988
Tantra: The Art of Conscious Loving	by	Charles a. Caroline Muir Mercury House Inc. San Francisco, 1989
Tantric Quest	by	Daniel Odier, Inner Traditions, Rochester,Vermont, 1997
The Thirteen Principal Upanishads	transl. by	R.E. Hume University Press, 2nd ed. rev. London, Oxford, 1931
Tools for Tantra	by	Harish Johari Destiny Books Vermont, 1986, 1st ed. 1934
The World of Tantra	by	B. Bhattacharya, Munshiram Manoharlal Publishers Pvt. Ltd. New Delhi, 1986

CPSIA information can be obtained
at www.ICGtesting.com
Printed in the USA
FFHW02n0128250818
47950745-51652FF